THE SHAMAN

NO GOOD DEED

D.L. LANGLEY

CHAPTER 1

Gabe Wakeman swung his heavy teak front door closed and tugged it to be sure the lock had set. He took a deep breath. He liked getting up early before the pull of the day's demands got hold of him. There was a mild onshore breeze, but the day promised to be hot. Dry leaves and twigs from the dense wall of tropical bamboo surrounding his house had collected on his Range Rover overnight. He liked the privacy the bamboo gave him but he was going to have to find time to chop it back before it engulfed his yard. He brushed the debris off his windshield and backed into the street.

The Southern California village of Seaside was a maze of shallow arroyos and narrow residential streets that snaked downhill to the town center. Gabe caught brief glimpses of the open ocean and railroad tracks paralleling the Pacific Coast Highway on his drive to Seaside's casual downtown – six square blocks of businesses catering to locals and tourists camping at the state beach.

He had arranged to meet his client, Vince Conklin, for breakfast at the Lonesome Threesome Bar and Grill. The TLT was a local hangout that had come to serve as Gabe's second office. He nosed into one of the parking spaces at the side of the building and cut the ignition. It was 6:30 and the restaurant wouldn't open for another half hour.

He shut his eyes and leaned back in his seat to get a sense of what would unfold in his meeting with Vince. Gabe shuddered and the sunlight dimmed. The image of a shadow within a shadow appeared in his mind. *Trouble was headed his way*.

Gabe had been experiencing altered states all of his life. His vision would suddenly shift as if a transparent overlay was projected upon the world. These glimpses opened his mind to unseen truths about people and he was more likely to respond to their energy than what they said. He had learned to hide these moments out of time from his family and the world, but Tip had taught him how to look with an unfocused mind to discern their meanings.

The CLOSED sign was still in the front window when he walked around the corner of the TLT, but Mac had unlatched the door and the aroma of frying bacon and fresh coffee greeted Gabe when he entered.

He'd wandered into the restaurant to get a sandwich when he moved to Seaside six years ago. The invisible hand of fate must have been directing him that day. He'd begun a conversation with one of the owners, Clare, that was still going on. His regular meetings with her created a break in his isolation and gave him a sense of clarity and direction.

Gabe was intrigued by the people who ran the TLT. He couldn't figure out how they fit together, but they felt like a family and their closeness soothed an abiding inner loneliness he didn't usually acknowledge.

Mac, the rumpled gray-haired patriarch was in the habit of giving unsolicited advice to patrons, whether they were listening or not. This morning he was deep in the morning crossword. Gabe seated himself at his usual window table and Clare appeared with a cup and a pot of coffee.

"Do you have time to join me?" he asked.

"I'd like to, but Sonny is taking Sylvie to the aquarium and I'm covering for him today." She filled his cup. "It's early. Are you meeting someone?"

"One of my favorite clients. Vince Conklin. You remember I helped get their son into rehab last year. Vince called and asked to meet him before work today. He has a problem with his godson and he thinks Journeywork will help him." Gabe didn't mention his flashback or the disquieting image of a double shadow. He knew Clare would eventually draw it out of him.

"You're reluctant." It was a statement, not a question. Clare was a willowy blonde with a disturbing habit of sensing Gabe's thoughts. He was attracted to her, but she'd been clear from the outset that romance was not on the menu. She'd become his confidante instead. She welcomed his visits but her life remained a mystery he couldn't penetrate.

"Vince is vulnerable to manipulation. He's big-hearted and he hires parolees and people out of rehab. But some people aren't open to help and his godson may be one of his lost causes."

"That challenge sounds perfect for you," her grin was sly. "Let's talk about it when we meet on Saturday." She topped off Gabe's cup and went to the open kitchen where Sonny and Chuy were singing Mexican ranchera ballads over the clatter of pots and pans.

Being a Shaman was Gabe's work, and in a deeper sense, his identity. Guide, teacher, witchdoctor, healer. Ancient titles for a calling as relevant today as it had been for millennia. Gabe used counseling and psychedelic plants to help people find their spiritual center and make lasting changes in their lives. His private practice was busy and he facilitated quarterly Journey Groups on Friday and Saturday evenings. He lived with the constant pressure of phone calls and texts from clients, many of whom forgot he was their Shaman and not a personal coach.

Vince Conklin parked his dusty black Cayenne with a WYCO 1 vanity plate at the curb outside the window and strode into the TLT in a swirl of hyperactivity. He was a burly, weatherworn man in his early fifties with a decisive jaw, long nose, and thinning black crewcut salted with gray. He waved to Mac and made a beeline to Gabe's table. Gabe had been working with Vince and his wife, Shelly for several years. They were high school sweethearts whose marriage was strained. They had a daughter in graduate school, but they'd never agreed on how to raise their troubled twenty-year-old son, Chad, and they were struggling with the fallout.

Vince's handshake was raspy and perfunctory. He was a successful land developer and multitasking was his norm, but today he looked like he was juggling too many balls and was about to drop one. He pulled out the chair facing Gabe and sat down with a nervous sigh.

"Thanks for meeting me on such short notice, Gabe. I called you because I'm worried about my godson, Bobby Wyring. He's my foreman on the Four Square Ranch project. We've got a hundred and twenty new homes going up and thirty days to get the models open. I put Bobby in charge because he's a can-do guy who thinks fast and gets things done. But he's not bird-dogging our suppliers the way he should and he's making mistakes that are costing us money."

"Slow down, Vince. I take it there's a reason you haven't fired him? Gabe experienced Vince's anxiety as a pressure lodged between his solar plexus and his heart.

"Bobby is family, Gabe. His mother owns half the business. His father, George, helped me get started thirty years ago. We built the company together. Wyring-Conklin is still a partnership even though George died in 2002. His wife, Mildred, owns half the business, and Bobby and his sister are in line to inherit.

"George expected Bobby to follow in his footsteps. Chad isn't interested or capable, so Bobby's our company's only hope. He has a head for the business and I've been mentoring him as best I can. But lately he's falling apart. I don't think his heart is in it. He completely missed our meeting with the subs this morning."

"Hungry, gentlemen? The kitchen is open." Clare appeared with a coffee pot and menus.

"'I'll have the special," Gabe said.

"One plate of Three Alarm Huevos."

"Make it two," Vince paused to admire Clare's figure as she glided toward the kitchen. "Bobby's marriage is in trouble."

"How old is he?"

"Thirty-five. He and Jessica got married out of college and they have two nice kids. I'd hate to see them split up. Jessica says he's moody and gambling too much. I worry about drugs."

Bobby sounded like an evolving train wreck to Gabe. "Has he ever been on antidepressants?"

"No, I suggested it but he refuses to go to a shrink."

"And he's not suicidal?"

"No way. I know this kid, Gabe. He's headed for trouble. You've done wonders for me and Shelly and you're the only one who can help Bobby. If you let him come to our Journey Group this Friday, you'll get to know him and I'm sure you can point him in the right direction."

Gabe felt the weight of Vince's expectations and wondered how *Gabriel Wakeman Saver of Lost Souls* would look on a business card. Clients came to him seeking relief from deep psychological pain that didn't respond to conventional treatments. Many had no idea he was healing their spirit as well as their psyche. He would talk to Bobby for Vince's sake, but he was no magician.

"I need to interview him before I invite him to your Group," Gabe temporized.

"Thanks, that's all I ask." Vince whipped his phone out of his pocket before Gabe could say more. "I'll send him your number."

"Two orders of Three Alarm Huevos." Clare unloaded her tray and set a ramekin of Chuy's Nuclear Salsa on the table between them. "Add this at your own risk," she warned. "It looks harmless but it can burn you."

CHAPTER 2

Gabe's compulsive need for privacy was memorialized in the rules for clients visiting his home. They were welcome in his living room, kitchen, and the guest bedroom and bath. The rest of his house was off-limits.

His home was a compact single-story block structure hidden behind a wall of thirty-foot bamboo. The garage, a windowless front door, and a gravel path into the foliage were all that was visible from the street. The path wound through the bamboo to a wide patio of rosy flagstone along the south side of Gabe's house. A lattice built under the eaves sheltered a workbench and his prized collection of bonsai trees. There were two chaise lounges on the patio with thick canvas cushions. A gnarled Australian willow canted above the flagstone and cast lacy shade on a weathered teak table and the cushioned chairs that lived there year-round.

Gabe brushed off the chairs and put two sweating bottles of cold water on the table in preparation for his meeting with Bobby Wyring. It was eight in the morning and the August sun was already stifling. The flock of goldfinches that lived in his garden had retreated to the deep shade of the bamboo. He listened to their melodic whistling to clear his mind.

Bobby arrived on time. Gabe heard his feet crunching on the gravel and watched him bound up the patio steps in one stride. Gabe's first encounter with a client was a critical moment that gave him a psychic print of the person — a clean gestalt — before the interpersonal field was muddled by familiarity.

Bobby was strikingly handsome in person. Blond and tall, about Gabe's height. Khaki shorts, work shoes, a clean blue WYCO construction T-shirt, and Oakleys on a leather keeper around his neck. His skin was sunbeaten and his loose shirt hid a softening waistline.

"Gabe Wakeman?" he offered his hand.

"You must be Bobby. It's good to meet you." Bobby's handshake was strong and callused. No wedding ring.

"We can sit out here," Gabe gestured at the table. A small bald spot was visible on the top of Bobby's head when he sat down.

"Vince wants me to talk to you about coming to his Group." Bobby's eyes were a piercing China blue. "He thinks I need it." His smile was dismissive.

"And do you?" Gabe's tone was light. "What do you want to change in your life?" Bobby didn't expect his direct question. Gabe saw him searching for an acceptable answer.

"Land development isn't exactly my dream job. It's something I inherited. Vince sees me as a partner someday." He shifted his chair a few inches back from the table, "But I don't know if it's what I want and I can't talk to him about it."

"Everything you say here is in confidence, Bobby. Vince may have sent you, but your private thoughts are safe with me. I don't share secrets." Gabe absorbed the sadness and longing

8

hidden under Bobby's personable façade. He let the silence stretch between them.

"Okay, if you want to know the truth, I feel trapped. Jess and I got married too young. We met when we were going to Santa Linda State. I used to surf at Pinos Riscos and she was the hottest girl on the beach. We got married after graduation. She'd done some modeling and wanted to be on TV so she auditioned to become the weather girl at Channel 8 but lost out to that Hawaiian girl on the evening news. She got a job selling commercials but that got boring fast, so then she wanted kids. Don't get me wrong – they're the best thing we ever did — Susan is seven and Jake is five – and Jess is a good mom but she's restless, resentful. Kinda sharp edged … like I'm the reason she's not famous. I work fifty hours a week and she goes shopping and gripes that I don't do my share at home."

Gabe didn't interrupt. He'd heard this story dozens of times. He wanted to see if Bobby would take responsibility for any of the problems in his life.

"We don't have anything in common except the kids." Bobby ran his thumbnail down the damp paper label on his water bottle and wadded up the strip. The plastic cap clicked as he twisted it off.

"You've been seeing other women." Gabe asserted.

"Yeah." Bobby looked up, surprised. "But none of them are serious. You know how it is — you meet a girl working for a supplier or a woman at the casino. Maybe married. No strings, just looking for a good time."

"What do you get out of it?"

"Fun. Release. But even that isn't helping lately."

"Does Jessica have affairs?"

"God no. She's too preoccupied with the kids."

"You mentioned the casino. How much do you gamble?"

"A little. I like it. Sometimes too much. But my gambling's not hurting Jess. If I come up short, I can always get money from Mother. That really pisses my sister, Dana off." Bobby grinned. There was mischief in his eyes, but no remorse. "She and Mother don't get along. Probably because they're too much alike. She thinks I'm the favorite."

"Are you?"

"I'm the son they always wanted." Bobby took a drink and set the bottle neatly in the wet ring it had made on the table. "I got plenty of attention but I've never felt like I belonged."

"Why not?"

"I'm adopted. Except for Jess, only my sister and our family housekeeper know. Dana is three years older. Mother couldn't get pregnant again so they adopted me."

"Vince doesn't know? He's your godfather."

"It's a big secret. I don't know how they managed to have Dana. They would have had to sleep together. Mother probably had rules about that. It's easy to see why Dana is such a complicated bitch. She was born mean, and nothing was ever her fault. Mother sent her to therapy but it only made her angrier. Our house was a damn war zone until she left for college."

Gabe imagined Bobby growing up in the Wyring household. Alienation carried into adulthood, driving him to medicate with casual sex and gambling. Gabe felt into his own experience to understand Bobby. He recalled the hollow echo of his father's footsteps on the hardwood floor of his childhood home. He'd grown up tough and self-reliant, joined ROTC in college and blindly followed his father into the Army. The military gave him an identity and a place to belong without the risk of emotional closeness.

If his helicopter hadn't crashed in Columbia he might never have found his own identity. The trauma kindled intense visions that Gabe's doctors at the VA tried to suppress with medication. He fell into a suicidal depression and would have killed himself if Dr. Joseph Tipton hadn't shaken him awake with a powerful combination of psychedelics and psychotherapy. Tip recognized his episodes as a rare talent and offered to teach him the art of Shamanism. Gabe apprenticed under Tip's relentless supervision for eight years before he began his own underground practice of Journeywork. Tip's mentorship had grown into a deep friendship.

"What has Vince told you about my work?" he asked Bobby.

"He says you give people psychedelics and they talk all night. Somehow that lets you see your life more clearly."

Gabe smiled at Bobby's description of Journeywork. It was like comparing a stroll in the park to a mountain climbing expedition. Guiding souls safely through the abyss of their unconscious required steady nerves, insight, and an intimate familiarity with your own demons.

"What's your history with psychedelics? Are you on any medications or have any health issues I should know about?"

"Nothing. A little pot. Shrooms a few times with friends and some cocaine back in college. I drink on weekends. That's it."

Gabe hadn't seen any indication of a mood disorder or the drug use Vince had mentioned. Bobby Wyring was emotionally immature but most men his age were. He was acting out the conflicts in his life instead of dealing with them and he hadn't cultivated any greater purpose than working and having fun.

Tipton had taught Gabe to see how clients handled medicine in a solo session before introducing them to Group work. Breaking protocol by letting him come to Vince's Group was a risk. But Bobby needed help now, and the next Group wouldn't meet for three months.

"All right, Bobby. The Group that Vince is in meets at his house tomorrow night. He will give you the details. Come ready to explore yourself in a new way."

CHAPTER 3

Gabe rang the bronze Acrosanti bell hanging by the front entrance of Joseph Tipton's cedar shingled ranch house and stepped back to appreciate the mottled afternoon shadows cast by a Torrey pine on the wide stone steps. Tip lived in Pinos Riscos, a few miles south of Seaside and Gabe felt welcome dropping in.

Tipton swung his door open with a book in one hand. His tall figure was slightly stooped and his eyes twinkled behind his wire-framed glasses. "Good to see you, Gabe. Come on in. I was reading on the patio and watching the light change. Would you like a beer?"

"Sounds good. I have a new client coming to Group I tomorrow night that I want to discuss."

Tip led Gabe through the open kitchen and collected two Coronas and a bag of pretzels on their way to the flagstone terrace overlooking the canyon at the back of the house. They clinked bottles and settled down to talk. Low afternoon sun lit the red rocks across the canyon. A dove cooed.

"You sound like you have doubts about this guy."

"Bobby Wyring. Vince Conklin is his godfather and he's pushing me to work with him. This will be his first Journey and I'd like a clearer sense of where he needs to go. Before I met Vince yesterday morning the image of a shadow within a shadow appeared in my mind. I felt cold.

"A warning?"

"Yeah. But I don't know what it means.

"What did you notice when you met with him?"

"He's thirty-five. Handsome and entitled. He says he feels like he doesn't belong and blames that on being adopted. He gambles too much and his mother bails him out. His marriage is a wreck; he's seeing other women. He's making mistakes on the job. I can't tell if he really wants to change or if he's coming to appease Vince."

"No sign of mania or mood disorder?"

"He's lonely, but I don't think he's depressed. He drinks, but no other signs of substance abuse."

"What does he hook in you, Gabe? How do you feel when you sit with him?"

"He went into the family business to please his father. That echoes my own story. He reminds me of how I used to be before my accident, before I started my work with you. Bobby's banging around, playing a role in a script he didn't write. I won't let my issues distort the interpersonal field. This is his life."

"It sounds like he's using anything possible to avoid necessary decisions. He'll resist admitting his deeper issues. He's going to test you."

"Do you think I'm wasting my time? He may be one of those people who wants to bump along the surface of life."

"You can't help everyone, but if you don't give him a chance and really engage him, he will never change," Tip said.

"Either you commit fully or you give him a nice experience in Journeyspace and send him on his way."

"I think I'll start him on a low dose of MDMA and see how he does."

"How do you think he'll mix with the other Group members?"

"I think he'll gravitate to Rudy and Jason. They're close to his age. Jackson is pretty wrapped up in Catherine's MS. If the new woman, Samantha Gresham, comes, he's likely to evade his problems by flirting with her."

"Let me know how it goes," Tip said.

CHAPTER 4

Journeywork attracted people seeking relief from physical or psychological problems that hadn't responded to conventional treatments. Reputable research, popular podcasts, and Michael Pollan's book, *Changing Your Mind*, had softened cultural mores about psychedelics and moved their use closer to the mainstream. People came to Gabe from all walks of life in search of personal growth. Gabe discouraged thrill seekers, but some of his clients were secretly hoping for a shortcut to god.

Gabe's Santa Linda Group I met quarterly at Vince Conklin's sprawling hillside estate three miles inland from the picturesque chain of beach towns strung along the Coast Highway north of Santa Linda. A wide drive flanked with queen palms led to a paved plaza in front of a sprawling Mediterranean style house with a gray tiled roof and acre of walled garden. The sun was tipping toward the horizon and there were several cars parked in the forecourt when Gabe arrived.

Group I had been meeting for six years. With Gabe's guidance they'd learned to navigate altered states of consciousness to touch the sacred and expand their understanding of themselves. They had been fasting all day and were putting away food for tomorrow's breakfast when Gabe came in and greeted them.

Vince had arranged futons in the spacious great room and people trailed in with blankets, pillows, water bottles, and notebooks.

Each year Gabe developed a theme, divided into four parts, to use with his quarterly Groups: Austin, New York, L.A., and two in Santa Linda. The theme provided a focus for the Group, but he never knew how the evening would go. Facilitation was like skiing or surfing - conditions were constantly changing. Plant medicines produced powerful unexpected emotions and Gabe's job was to guide Journeyers safely across shifting terrain.

With Bobby there were ten people in the Group tonight. Diane Viscalia, a low-key hospice nurse, who used Journeywork to strengthen her capacity to comfort the dying had brought her friend, Samantha Gresham, for the second time. Sam was a tall, sexy, ambivalently divorced veterinarian, with smoky gray eyes and a ready smile that Gabe found alluring.

Vince, Rudy Mayer, and Bobby were seated together. Gabe noticed Bobby had angled his body so he had a clear view of Sam.

Rudy owned the Holistic Rainbow Clinic in Old Palmitas. He was a chiropractor and talented acupuncturist who treated Gabe for chronic back and shoulder pain. Rudy was gregarious and open-hearted. They'd developed a casual friendship that involved regular beach runs and an occasional beer. Appearances mattered to him and his wardrobe was carefully curated. The ruby stud in his left ear was a bid to impress his new girlfriend.

Jackson Aldridge was a millennial techie who'd dropped out of MIT and invented an Internet protocol that optimized key search terms for targeted advertising. He'd cashed out for $300 million dollars and was determined to spend his fortune philanthropically. His arm was wrapped protectively around his wife, Catharine. She suffered from MS evinced by a slow deterioration with rare episodes affecting her strength and mobility. They wanted to conceive but were understandably anxious about the risks. Gabe often caught Catharine staring at death and hiding her fears from Jackson.

Jill Newsome and Brian Klingmeyer would be a couple if one of them dared express a hidden attraction to the other. Jill was a cushiony expressive arts therapist who had been sexually abused in her teens. She dressed in flamboyant, provocative clothes that contradicted her fear of men. Journeywork had allowed her to explore her buried shame, and at fifty, she was finding her way to a new identity. Brian was an anthropology professor at Santa Linda State who'd spent more time immersed in the ancient past than relating to others. His professional preoccupation had cost him his marriage, but he was finding the courage to make eye contact with Jill.

Jason De Veaux completed the Group. Jason was an insecure thirty-eight-year-old African-American musician who made his living scoring video games. He was artfully tattooed and had a habit of calling Gabe about decisions in his life.

There was an electric hum in the air beneath the burble of conversation as people got settled. Gabe took the chair Vince had set out for him and began tonight's theme: *Disowned Voices* — the second installment of the year's motif on identity.

"We experience our moment to moment reality as continuous—like a movie. But we unconsciously shift between different aspects of ourselves — our sub-personalities — in order to adapt to changing situations." The room grew silent as

Gabe spoke. "These sub-personalities have distinct voices. They protect us and keep us in line. When there's too much stress or trauma we disown some of our voices in order to survive."

Gabe looked around the room and thought of each person's disowned voices. Vince had been roughed up by his alcoholic father and disowned his aggression. He'd never resolved the issue and hadn't learned how to set limits with his wife, and son, Chad. He believed in giving people second chances and hired ex-cons on his jobsites. Gabe planned to give him ayahuasca tonight and catch him in the third hour when he'd be open to feeling his suppressed rage. Dianne's engagement with her dying patients' denials of death resulted in her minimizing her own grief. She had some crying to do. Sam was new and Gabe was curious about her. He was going to continue her on 2CB until he had a clearer picture of her psyche. Rudy Mayer's disowned shame originated from envy of his older brother, a medical doctor whom his parents idealized. Gabe would give Rudy MDMA and work with him to internalize his own value. Gabe decided to start Bobby on a lower dose of the same substance and pair him with Rudy.

When Gabe had finished the introduction, each person in turn voiced their intention for the evening. He administered the medicines in reverent silence. Jackson followed Jason through the sliding doors into the starlit garden and the others got comfortable on the futons. Gabe started gentle music to ease the travelers through the bumpy hour of transition into altered states of consciousness.

Vince, Jill, and Brian were cocooned in blankets, deep in their ayahuasca visions. Sam and Diane sensed Catharine's unvoiced fear and drew her into an empathetic huddle. Gabe listened to the murmuring rise and fall of their voices, as much for the tone as their words. Sam was wearing workout leggings and a summer tee and the lamplight outlined the graceful shape of her body. Their heads were close together. They felt peaceful and Gabe knew they were helping each other.

People make sense of themselves and the world by forming closed loops of thought, feeling, and meaning. Psychedelic substances break the loops open and throw people into a place of confusion. Reality disintegrates. They are free to view life from a different angle and construct new meanings. A Shaman's job is to guide Journeyers safely through the jumbled psychedelic landscape toward a more complete identity.

Gabe closed his eyes and tuned into his own deepest disowned voice: a little boy who marched to his father's expectations in order to feel loved but abandoned himself in the process. Gabe felt the ancient ache of longing in his chest. Accessing his personal pain would resonate in the interpersonal field and shift the Group's members deeper into themselves. Who else in the room had a similar experience other than Bobby? Brian's face appeared in Gabe's mind. He looked in his direction and saw Brian shake off the blankets and sit up. Gabe went over to him and put his hand on his shoulder. "What are you noticing?"

"The ayahuasca is showing me how I wall myself off." He covered his eyes with his hands. "I'm so lonely …" Brian began to sob.

Gabe didn't move. His silence created an empathic space for Brian to experience the depth of his sorrow.

"I couldn't throw a baseball when I was a kid and there was no one to teach me. I didn't fit in. So, I studied. That made me good in school, but nobody liked me.

"I married the first girl who paid attention to me. I thought we were okay because we never fought. Before she left me, she said that I didn't know how to express my feelings. She was right. I've been hiding all my life." Brian paused to blow his nose. "I studied anthropology because the past felt safe. But I never learned to be myself with living people. I've wasted all this time."

"You have a lifetime of tears to shed, Brian. You've kept this loneliness and longing for connection with others hidden from yourself for decades. That's yours to feel. Don't be ashamed of the pain and don't be ashamed of your need to belong." Brian sank back into his blankets.

Gabe sensed a sudden disturbance in the flow of energy in the room, an invisible wave of heat and color buffeted him. Rudy motioned to Gabe, signaling concern. He and Bobby were engaged in animated conversation. Gabe went over and sat down next to them. "How are you feeling?" he asked Bobby. He took his hand; it was moist. Bobby's pupils were huge and he had a slight tremor in both hands. His reaction was disproportionate to the small dose of substance Gabe had given him.

"I feel wonderful! I'm flying. But I'm kinda jittery. Is this normal? My heart is beating in my ears and I can't finish my thoughts."

"He's been talking really fast and I'm having trouble keeping up," Rudy said.

"Hey Gabe!" Jason burst into the room. There's somebody sneaking around in the garden! He's a big guy. Jackson saw him too."

"Excuse me," Gabe said. "You two okay for a minute?"

"Yeah, man. I got it," Rudy said.

Bobby nodded, but elation and panic were close cousins, and Gabe knew Bobby could flip into fear. He needed to be grounded.

"I won't be long," he told Rudy, "Stay with him. I need to take care of this."

"We caught a glimpse of him, but it's easy to lose someone out here." Jason followed Gabe.

"Go back inside and stay there until I have a look," Gabe told him. "Where's Jackson?"

"He went around by the tennis court."

"If he comes back, keep him inside."Gabe followed the flagstone path away from the light. Unobtrusive solar markers outlined the paths and manicured bushes loomed motionless in the summer dark. Gabe paused every few steps to listen. There was a clunk to his left; he turned toward it, poised. A raccoon waddled into view, gave him an alarmed look and kept moving. Gabe let out his breath and pushed into the landscaping in the direction the raccoon had appeared from.

The bushes to his left erupted. The sour fug of beer filled his nose and Gabe was thrown forward by a solid whack on his back. He hit the ground and rolled reflexively, leaping upright, ready to fight. He saw the scissor of legs pass in front of the ground lights, running toward the front wall of the garden. Gabe ignored the burning pain of the blow and launched himself after the intruder.

"Gabe, come here! We need your help!" Rudy was frantic.

"I'm coming!" Gabe pivoted and turned back to the house. His attacker was getting away but he had to be sure his clients were safe.

"Are you okay?" Jackson ran up to Gabe panting. "I saw him run past me and climb over the wall to the driveway. Whoever it was is gone. It's really strange. This place is so private."

"Bobby, stop! You can't drive!" Gabe heard Rudy shouting in the driveway and a squeal of tires. Gabe and Jackson ran through the house and burst out the front door in time to see the taillights of Bobby's silver Sequoia vanish into the night.

"He went paranoid on me and I couldn't hold him!" Rudy was desperate. He grabbed Gabe's arm. "The guy was completely crazy. I tried to calm him down, but he kept insisting that he wasn't safe here. He said that guy in the garden was going to kill him!"

CHAPTER 5

Gabe led them back inside and tried to project a sense of calm while suppressing his fear about Bobby on substance, manic, and driving in the darkness. Fortunately, the Group members trusted him to take care of the situation and remained absorbed in their own experiences, unaware that there had been an emergency.

Everyone eventually went to bed except Gabe, whose anxiety about Bobby had weaponized his chronic insomnia. He'd taken a risk by letting Bobby into a Group before evaluating him in an individual session and now he was in danger. Bobby's reaction to the small dose of MDMA didn't make sense. He called his cell again without getting an answer.

At seven in the morning the Group was up making a communal breakfast. Gabe and Vince excused themselves and went into Vince's study to call Bobby's wife.

"Jessica?"

"Yes?" Her voice was seductive.

"This is Gabe Wakeman. Bobby came to a meeting I facilitated at Vince's house last night and left unexpectedly. I've been trying to reach him on his cell. Is he with you?"

"No," she paused again. "He said he was going to some self-improvement thing at Vince's and not to expect him home before noon today. Or he could have been lying. My sister-in-law, Dana, saw him having dinner in Welsprings with some blonde last Wednesday. Maybe he's with her." She didn't bother to disguise her anger.

"It sounds like Bobby's been doing things that are hurting you. Is there anything you can tell me that will help me find him?"

"Did he tell you about our marriage? He goes his own way and I take care of the kids."

Gabe thought he heard a muffled laugh in the background.

"Look, Bobby is not a bad man. But he needs to grow up. He's been depressed for months and he's been using crystal meth to pick himself up. I don't suppose he told you *that*."

Gabe cursed silently. He wouldn't have given Bobby anything if he had known he was abusing crystal. Methedrine causes paranoia and the MDMA on top of it was too much stimulant for him to handle. "Is he using any other drugs?"

"Not unless you count alcohol and gambling — and women."

Gabe ignored her snipe. "Do you know where he may have gone?"

"You could try Seaside." Jessica was impatient to get off the phone. "He said he was meeting a guy there tomorrow afternoon."

"Will you please have him call me when you see him? It's important that I talk with him."

"Yeah, *if* he comes home." There was a shrug in her voice.

###

Jessica ended the call and fell back on the rumpled bed into the welcoming arms of the man beside her. "Bobby took off and Vince is looking for him. God, I don't know how much more of his bullshit I can take! I'd like to chuck it all and run away with you."

CHAPTER 6

Gabe led the Group's Integration after breakfast. He listened attentively as each person recounted the insights and realizations they'd gleaned from the Journey. The Group was animated, but Gabe's back hurt where his attacker had walloped him and a purple bruise was forming as a painful reminder of his failure to recognize Bobby's impulsivity.

Jason needed to vent about the surprise of finding an intruder in the garden and Bobby's terrified flight. He told the story several times. Jackson regarded the incident as an exciting adventure, but Vince was uncharacteristically quiet. He'd pressured Gabe to take Bobby on and his good intention had blown up in his face. Rudy felt guilty that he hadn't been able to prevent Bobby from taking off. Brian was sitting next to Jill and whispered something to her that brought happy color to her face. Catharine had spent most of the evening communing with Diane and Sam. Her anguish had been visibly softened by their willingness to explore her fear of death with openness and empathy. Sam admitted to the Group that she still had confused feelings about her ex-husband and was working to sort them out. She spoke thoughtfully and Gabe felt a spark of connection each time their eyes met. He cautioned himself not to take it personally. Positive transferences were common after a Journey.

Gabe was relieved when the Integration was over. He'd never had a client tear out in the middle of a session before. He blamed himself for not reading Bobby correctly. The image of his tail lights disappearing into the night filled Gabe's mind. Why had Bobby imagined someone wanted to kill him? Was that the crystal talking? He wouldn't relax until he turned up safe.

He dragged home to shower before going to the TLT to eat and meet Clare. Mac and Chuy were churning out orders of the day's special when he arrived and Mac's chatty better half, Mom, was waiting tables with Sonny.

The TLT had once been a bowling alley and Mac had continued buying up adjacent properties over the years until he owned most of the block. He and Mom lived in an apartment above the restaurant. The Annex along the side street was dedicated to their only child, Sonny and his computers. Mac was a master repairman and he had converted an old garage in the alley into a shop that doubled as a clubhouse for his cronies. Clare lived in a cozy shingled cottage under a spreading live oak tree behind the restaurant with her precocious daughter, Sylvie.

Mac presided over the bar and kept a supply of paperback mysteries and board games stored underneath for the rare moments when he wasn't talking. All the regulars called Mac's wife Mom. Her fluffy white curls matched her trademark pearls. She looked harmless but her cheerful way of disarming people made her more effective than a bouncer.

Sonny home-schooled Clare's daughter, Sylvie, and worked the kitchen with Chuy, the chef. He was a child savant who had gotten a scholarship to Oxford at fifteen and developed a huge audience giving Dharma talks to interested students. When they started idealizing him, he left college to avoid becoming a cult figure, but Gabe wondered if he was still dispensing spiritual messages in the anonymity of the internet.

Sonny turned from the table he was attending and saluted with his coffeepot. Gabe felt oddly comforted by the gesture.

Mom brought Gabe's order. He downed a creamy bowl of Chuy's Guilty Gazpacho and a side of basil bruschetta without tasting them and exited through the kitchen to the shaded courtyard behind the TLT.

Clare was digging weeds from a raised vegetable box. She waved and peeled off her gloves and broad brimmed hat.

"Whew. It's hot. I'm glad to stop. Take a chair under the tree and I'll bring us some ice tea."

Gabe sank into one of the faded chairs in the dry shade of the live oak and propped his feet on the edge of the tiled fountain. He watched jays swooping for water and he felt his body begin to relax.

"Here we are." Clare returned with a sweating pitcher and two cold glasses with lemon slices in them. "How did last night go?"

"It was a mess. Vince brought his godson, Bobby Wyring. I gave Bobby a small dose of MDMA and that would have been all right, but he'd been doing meth and hadn't told me. Some of the other Group members discovered a man hiding in the garden. I chased him and he clobbered me from behind. Bobby went nuts and took off in his truck, yelling that the guy wanted to kill him."

"That sounds pretty wild. Are you okay?"

"A little bruised. I haven't slept much. But I never do. Vince is blaming himself for pressuring me to bring Bobby into the Group. He was very quiet at Integration this morning."

"Who attacked you?"

"No idea, he hit me from behind. Jason and Jackson described him as a large dark man. That's too generic to be useful. I'm worried about Bobby. What if he gets into an accident or hurts himself?"

"You were trying to help him and he panicked. That wasn't your fault."

"It was my duty to keep him safe."

"You feel guilty even though you did your best to protect him. Why did Bobby come to you?"

"He's bored in his marriage and lost in distractions. He's not performing on the job. He gambles and does drugs. His wife thinks he's having an affair. He thinks the source of all his trouble is outside himself. He's carried a sense of alienation since his childhood because he's adopted and he's never stopped to think about who he really is."

"Um-hum," Clare said. "Any idea where he might be?"

"He hasn't been home. I called his wife and she sounds like she doesn't care. She says he's supposed to meet someone here in Seaside tomorrow. I'll look for him then."

"The Seaside Surf Fair is this weekend. The town will be overrun with tourists."

"Great. I need a bigger haystack." Gabe's phone chimed and he tipped the screen so Clare could see it. "It's Vince," Gabe said. "Maybe he's found him."

"Gabe, Bobby just called me. He sounded manic. He wouldn't listen to reason. He says he's not coming back to work. Ever. He asked about other psychedelic groups in the area but I told him I don't know any and I wouldn't tell him if I did. He said he'd find one on his own if I didn't help him. I tried to get him to call you, but no go."

"You did the right thing, Vince. I'm getting a treatment from Rudy Mayer later today— he knows everyone. I'll ask him if he knows of a Journey Group where Bobby might show up. Either way, I'm going to look for Bobby here in Seaside tomorrow. I'll text you if I find him."

Gabe ended the call and turned to Clare. "Now what? I have commitments to other people. I can't put my life on hold to hunt for Bobby. I'm supposed to fly to Sacramento on Wednesday to do a private session with Wes Keeler." Weston Keeler was a highly ethical state senator who struggled with the compromises of political life and regularly sought Gabe's counsel.

"Postpone your meeting with Senator Weston," Clare suggested. "You need to be here right now."

He knew she was right. He didn't like to cancel sessions, but he wouldn't rest easy until Bobby turned up.

Gabe was getting in his car when his phone chimed again. It was Sam Gresham asking him to meet for coffee. They settled on Tuesday evening at the TLT. He remembered the sexual jolt he'd felt when their eyes met, but Tip had taught him not to confuse a client's needs with his own. What was on her mind?

CHAPTER 7

Sunday morning dawned hot and stifling. The news was filled with reports of trail closures due to triple digit temperatures and imminent fire danger. There was a power outage in the East County. Everyone had turned their air conditioner on at once and overwhelmed the grid.

The sliding doors and windows were open at Tip's home when Gabe rapped lightly on the doorframe and walked in. Newspapers were strewn on the patio table and Tip's wife, Margaret, was reading the arts section in the New York Times. Tip was scrambling eggs in the kitchen.

"Come in, Gabe, and help yourself to coffee," Tip said. "I'll have these ready by the time the toast pops. There's fresh OJ in the fridge if you want some. How did Friday night go?"

Gabe got a coffee mug and juice glass and filled them. "It was ... difficult. I'd like to talk about it with both of you when we sit down. Mags may have some helpful insights."

Gabe took a swig of his juice and carried his cup and glass out to the patio. Mags was a clinical psychologist and one of Gabe's favorite people. She and Tip had been married for decades and she maintained a busy practice from their home.

"Good morning, Gabe." Mags folded her paper as he bent to kiss her cheek. "You look tired. Not sleeping again?"

"I had a rough session Friday and I could use some advice."

Tip appeared with a platter of toast and a pan of eggs and bacon. "Let's eat first, while the food is hot,"

"Hot!" Mags chuckle was musical. "This summer is the hottest I can remember since we moved here. Fire warnings are coming earlier every year." She tucked a wisp of snowy hair into her neat chignon and passed an orange pill bottle to Tip with one hand and a plate to Gabe with the other. "Eat up, young man. I want to hear about your session. Take your pill, Joseph."

"What's going on?" Gabe asked.

"He's been having runs of atrial fibrillation and doesn't like to admit he needs medication," Mags said.

"That damn med makes me tired. I'm not sure I need it." Tip protested. He shook a pill out of the bottle and swallowed it as Mags watched.

"Go on with your story," she said.

Gabe was concerned about Tip's health, but he didn't think he was willing to discuss it. He related the events of Friday night between bites. "Finding an intruder in the garden really set Bobby off."

"It's likely that the Ecstacy combined with the crystal to kindle Bobby's paranoia." Tip said. "MDMA is a useful tool to open the heart but adding it to meth is like pouring gasoline on a fire."

"His behavior could be a manic defense against anxiety, Mags said. "Something in his early relationships compromised his attachments. He made career and marriage decisions from an incomplete sense of self. His life must feel like it belongs to someone else."

"Could there be a personal link between Bobby and the man in the garden? Any idea who he was?" Tip asked.

"No clue. It was strange – Vince's place is very private. I was looking for the guy but he hit me from behind and fled. Jackson said he was a big man, but it was too dark to see his face."

"What are you going to do, Gabe?" Tip asked.

"Bobby's wife said he has a meeting in Seaside this afternoon. If he doesn't surface, I'll look for him there."

CHAPTER 8

Gabe left Tipton's house in Pinos Riscos and jumped on the I-5 past Seaside to the next beach town north. Old Palmitas boasted five stoplights and an Amtrak station. Its funky shopping district specialized in New Age bookstores, resale clothing boutiques, and upscale bars posing as restaurants. A dilapidated movie theatre that reeked of marijuana and the pristine domes of the Lotus Mind Fellowship bookended the town.

The Holistic Rainbow Clinic was on a side street one block west of the main drag. A cheerful hand painted sign depicting a double rainbow emerging from a froth of white clouds arched above the entrance of the two-story frame structure. Rudy Mayer owned the building and rented the spaces he didn't use for his chiropractic practice to a colorful collection of alternative practitioners. He was an expert acupuncturist who believed all physical maladies resulted from blockages in energy flow.

The HRC was quiet on a Sunday afternoon. Rudy had left the front door ajar and was straightening brochures and racks of aromatherapy bottles in the cluttered reception area. He snapped on the lights and waved Gabe down the corridor to his treatment room. "Come on in and shut the door. Bobby flipping out like that isn't good for the tension you carry in your back."

"I hope you can help me find him." The familiar menthol scent of Tiger Balm in Gabe's nostrils promised relief.

Rudy took a critical look at Gabe's posture. "You're tilting to the left. Let's start face down. Try to relax."

"That's hard to do when Bobby's in the wind and my back is nagging at me." Gabe removed his shirt and stretched out on the table.

"Wow. What happened? You've got a lot of bruising going on here."

"The guy in the garden hit me."

"Looks like he used something heavy. By the color of the bruise it really hurt. And of course, you didn't mention it."

Rudy turned on some soft music, draped a flannel sheet over Gabe and began inserting warmed needles into his neck. "That was wild, him driving off like that." He twisted the needles and Gabe flinched. "He hasn't shown up yet? How can I help?"

"Bobby called Vince yesterday trying to find more Journey Groups. You know everybody in the county. Any idea where he might have gone?"

"I know a couple in Pinecrest who hold an event every Saturday. Darin Red Deer claims to be a quarter Yaqui. He drives a skip loader during the week and helps his wife Shakti run psychedelic Rituals on weekends. She's an artist who's amazing with tarot and numerology."

Amazing, the New Age catch-all for everything from hamburgers to mystical experiences. Gabe was skeptical of tarot, numerology, and the healing powers of crystals, but they worked for Rudy so he kept his judgement to himself.

"This will help your spasms. Try to relax." Rudy held the soles of Gabe's feet with his hands in silence before he removed the needles. "That should feel better." He allowed Gabe to sit up and put on his shirt. "Let's call Shakti and see if she's heard from Bobby." Rudy found Shakti's name in his contacts and called while Gabe listened.

"Namaste, Shakti, this is Rudy Mayer, you remember me from the Energy Healing Workshop in Santa Fe? We're on speaker with my friend Gabe Wakeman. He's my shaman." Rudy explained what had happened with Bobby and asked if she had heard from him.

"The new guy. Wow. I had *no* idea. He was here last night. He seemed okay. He spent most of the time with my friend, Deva, and left this morning. I don't know where he went but I'm holding a Ritual here next Saturday and he asked if he could come. It's, like, open to everyone, so I said sure."

Gabe spoke up. "Shakti, this is Gabe Wakeman. Bobby came to my Group on Saturday night and took off in a manic state. He's using crystal and he shouldn't be taking any psychoactive substances. I'm hoping to find him today, but if I don't, would it be okay for me to come to your Ritual next Saturday to talk him down?"

"That's chill. Sounds like he's stuck in his second chakra. Crystal is evil stuff and we don't want it here. Darin and I are happy to help."

Rudy thanked her and ended the call. "This can't be helping your insomnia or your shoulder pain, Gabe. Don't you have a friend who is a sheriff's detective?"

"Marco Brandt, but this isn't a matter for the police. Bobby's wife says he has an appointment in Seaside this afternoon. Maybe I'll find him."

"Good luck with that. The Seaside Surf Fair is on. It's going to be a mob scene."

CHAPTER 9

The Coast Highway had slowed to a crawl. Gabe got off the main drag and zigzagged through residential neighborhoods to get back to his home in Seaside. The streets in the center of town were cordoned off to traffic, so he parked at home and walked down the hill to look for Bobby.

The Annual Seaside Surf Fair featured several bands and drew visitors from all over the county. The reverb of speaker systems and instruments sailed over the noise of the crowd. Gabe pushed through the milling throng searching for Bobby. Suntanned girls in thong bikinis and tattooed men in board shorts and flip-flops spilled off the sidewalks into the streets. Some of them were already wasted. Venders were selling food and souvenirs from booths set up beneath the hundred-year-old eucalyptus trees in the town park.

"Gabe! Yoo-hoo! Over here!"

He turned at the sound of his name. Shelly Conklin, Vince's wife, was waving from a booth decorated with a green and white SPAY YOUR PET banner. He waved and walked over to meet her.

"You know my son, Chad. He and his friend, Hayley, are volunteering today." Shelly looked proud and nervous at the same time. Chad was a late life baby who was a headache for his parents. His sister was pursuing a degree in electrical engineering but Chad was living at home with nine months of sobriety.

Hayley was a painfully thin dishwater blonde with green Jello streaks in her hair and a Barbie face. She cast a flirtatious look at Gabe. Chad grunted and offered his hand. He had a slight build and cocky posture. His eyes were sleepy and he hadn't shaved in a while.

"I hear you're working for your father this summer," Gabe said.

"Yeah." Chad deadpanned. "And I gotta be here on my day off."

"He's just saying that," Shelly injected. "He really loves animals, and I'm so glad you do too, sweetie." She included Hayley in her enthusiasm.

Hayley ignored the endearment and rolled her eyes, "Yeah, right. He, like, *loves* to volunteer."

"You haven't seen Bobby Wyring around have you?" Gabe asked them.

Chad shook his head no.

"I'm so worried about him," Shelly said. "Vince told me what happened. I'll call you if I do."

"We gotta go, Mom. I promised I'd meet some guys," Chad snapped.

"Be sure and take some water, honey, you too, Hayley," she called as they walked away. "It's so hot out."

Gabe spent another exhausting hour searching for Bobby, but finding him in the crowd was hopeless and he retreated to the TLT for an early dinner.

39

Mac refused to allow any electronic devices in the TLT except for phones – with the ringer off. The comparative quiet was a relief even though the place was jumping. The lights were soft after the glare outdoors. Air from the ceiling fans fluttered the leaves of the green plants hanging between the windows. Mac's buddies, Big Wave O'Shea and Duke the Cabbie were installed on their usual stools with a row of empties lined up like soldiers in front of them. Gabe clapped them on the back in greeting as he walked by.

"Hi, Mr. Wakeman, are you enjoying the Fair?" Clare's eight-year-old daughter, Sylvie, was perched at the kitchen-end of the bar folding origami animals out of brightly colored paper. Marlowe, her spotted cat, scrutinized each creation as intently as if it might sprout whiskers and run away. Gabe took a seat next to her where he could survey the tables and upholstered booths at the far end of the room while he waited for a table to free up.

"I'm looking for someone, but it's very loud out there and I thought I'd take a break. Is your mother here?"

"She's away. Sonny is babysitting us. Not that we actually *need* a sitter. We're not going to wander onto the train tracks or get lost." Marlowe rubbed a tawny ear against Gabe's arm in agreement.

Mac interrupted their conversation and plunked a cold bottle of Effable Ale in front of Gabe. "Ya look tired and hungry, Gabe. What'll it be?"

"What's the special?"

Mac's eyes lit up. "Eventuality Eggplant or Redemption Ratatouille."

"How are they different?"

"There *is* no difference." Mac chortled. "They're identical. Sonny just likes to see which customers choose which dish."

"Since it doesn't matter," Gabe tipped his bottle, "I'll take Redemption."

CHAPTER 10

Chad used his fake ID to get into the roped off beer garden. He bought a pair of drafts and sneaked them outside the ropes. He handed one to Hayley and they climbed on top of a dumpster to take in a set from a local R & B band. He hoped he'd spot some of his usual customers in the crowd. They'd vaped earlier, but his high was wearing off, and when Hayley came down, she'd be ragging him about letting her in on his business now that she was having his baby.

"Want another hit?" he took a drag and offered her the vape pen.

"Yeah, what I'd really like is a couple of lines."

"Later, babe. I gotta check in at the booth and there's business to do. We got all night and we don't want to peak too soon." Hayley shrugged and took out her lipliner. She applied a coat of candied gel and invited him to taste it.

They were nodding to the music when he spotted his construction boss, Jack Harrar, in the crowd. Sick. Harrar was the kind of man Chad wanted to be. He was totally buffed. His seen-everything vibe had a tortured undercurrent that drew women like sugar.

They had an unspoken arrangement. Chad sold Harrar drugs and in return, Harrar kept Bobby off his back and let him dog it on the job site. He talked a smooth line that Chad envied. But you wouldn't want to fuck with him. There was a rumor that he'd killed a man when he was in prison.

Harrar might want a gram of crystal to up his game with the ladies. Chad stood up to wave at him and stopped. Hayley was grooving to the music and didn't notice. The dissonant wail of the northbound Coaster train cut through the music as it rumbled toward Seaside. Harrar's hair gleamed like jet as he leaned close to Bobby. Harrar grabbed Bobby in a bear hug. Bobby slumped against him and punched the air trying to break free. Harrar backed away and Bobby staggered and took off running toward the tracks.

What was this all about? Chad had seen Harrar hitting on Jessica Wyring at Bobby's company birthday bash a couple of months ago and Jessica being into it. Had Bobby found out? He jumped down from his perch enjoying the idea. Bobby was a dickhead who rode his ass on the job and Chad resented his dad using Bobby as an example of good behavior.

He tossed his empty beer cup toward the dumpster and heard it roll away. His mother would give him shit if they were gone from fucking Spay Your Pets too long.

CHAPTER 11

The sun was sliding toward the western horizon and well-oiled customers were spilling out of the beer garden onto the sidewalks when Gabe left the TLT. Several bands were competing for loudest place. Fans were dancing to the amplified racket as if it was a rave.

Gabe looked over the sea of bobbing heads.

Bobby appeared ten feet away; he was running. Or trying to. The dancers had linked arms in a swaying conga line that buffeted him back the way he'd come. Bobby looked over his shoulder, searching for something. Gabe shouted at Bobby and pushed toward him. The wall of dancers undulated and he managed to grab Bobby's arm.

"I've been looking for you!" Gabe shouted. Bobby gaped at Gabe without recognition and tried to yank free of his grasp. "We need to talk!"

Bobby's features liquified in front of Gabe's eyes as if he was ripping away a succession of masks distorted by terror and confusion Gabe recognized the surreal quality of the image as his own projection.

"I've got to get out of here!" Bobby wrenched free and ran.

Gabe followed, bumping into people and yelling his name over the clang of the warning bells at the railroad crossing. Bobby ran downhill toward the tracks. There was another shrill blast of the whistle. The ground shook underfoot. The red lights at the crossing were flashing and the warning bells were clanging. Bobby glanced back, but didn't slow down. He dodged around the zebra striped gate arm onto the tracks.

The train hit him with a terrible slowness. Gabe saw Bobby's body hurtle end over end and disappear. The engineer hit the brakes. Gabe registered the earsplitting squeal in the silence of his mind. Sparks flew from steel against steel. Someone screamed. The huge black engine loomed over Bobby's body like a great snake scraping him up, consuming him.

Rail cars rumbled by as the train ground to a halt. Passengers stared out of the lighted windows. A crowd gathered at the crossing gate. Women were crying. Gabe bent over with his hands on his thighs, taking deep breaths to steady himself. The band music faded in the background. Time was on hold.

He had to call Marco.

CHAPTER 12

The police arrived in minutes with sirens howling, and cordoned off the area on both sides of the train. A hushed throng gathered to gawk. The spectacle of death drew them like excited sharks. Daylight faded to darkness and flares were lit along a full block of track. Ambulances came and left and police cars splashed blue lights on the faces of stunned bystanders. Gabe stood alone at the edge of the cordon rocked by the complete unreality of the scene. He was hit with a flare of rage at the senselessness and waste of death. He'd seen death before. But he didn't expect to encounter it in civilian life. Had Bobby been running in a blind panic? Did he think he could cross the tracks ahead of the train? They'd never know.

He called Vince to give him the awful news while he waited to speak to his friend Marco.

"I don't understand! Bobby wouldn't do this!" Vince choked down a sob. "He has everything to live for."

"I tried to stop him but he took off running. I'm sorry, Vince."

"Why would he run? This makes no sense. He knows you."

"He yelled that he had to get away. I don't know what else to tell you."

"Oh god, I can't believe it. I'll have to tell Jessica. And Mildred. What will I say to them?" His voice broke.

"Nothing yet, Vince. Wait until the police are done. Are you going to be okay?"

"Yes, I guess so. Call me when you know something."

Gabe rang off and Sonny emerged from the crowd. "What happened?" he asked.

"My client, Bobby Wyring, ran in front of the train." Gabe heard the flatness of his own voice.

"My god, Gabe." Sonny's face expressed the horror Gabe wasn't ready to feel. "Is there any way I can help?"

"Thanks Sonny. I'll be okay." Gabe knew that wasn't true but he hoped Sonny would leave it alone. Sonny gave him a knowing look and patted him on the back.

"I have to go, Marco's here." Gabe waited by the barrier for Marco Brandt to finish talking with the cluster of sheriff's deputies who were directing the activity on the track before he strolled over to where Gabe was standing. They'd known one another since Marco was eighteen. He was fresh out of boot camp when he joined Gabe's unit. Marco served under Gabe's command in Columbia until he transferred stateside to get married. They met again by chance in Santa Linda, where Marco had moved to raise his family. He still wore his hair in a military cut, but there were threads of white in his dark hair and the stubble on his chin. He must be pushing forty. Gabe knew from their sparring practice at the dojo that his body was solid muscle.

"Hola, Wakeman. This is ugly. Not much of him to bury." The white suited CSI team was moving up and down the tracks setting up lights. "I hear you knew him?" Marco was dressed for a lazy Sunday at home.

47

"Bobby Wyring. I met him on Thursday and he came to my Group at Vince Conklin's on Friday night. Bobby is Vince's godson. He had been using crystal but didn't tell me. You'll find MDMA and meth in his blood. There was a trespasser in Vince's garden. Bobby bolted and I've been trying to find him."

"He's married?"

"Yes. His wife, Jessica, hasn't seen him since Friday, but she said he was meeting somebody here today and I came to look for him. I found Bobby, but he didn't recognize me and when I tried to grab him, he yelled, 'I've got to get out of here'. He broke loose and ran toward the tracks. He seemed disoriented."

"Where did you first spot him?"

"Up there in front of the bandstand," Gabe pointed uphill.

"Whoa. You've got blood on your shirt, amigo. Are you hurt?"

"No. I'm fine." Gabe pulled his shirt out and looked at the stain Marco was pointing to. He felt his side. "This isn't my blood."

"Don't wash that shirt, Wakeman, I'm going to need it. If it's Bobby's blood, it means he was injured before he ran into the train. Did you notice anything else?"

"He looked back at me when he was running and he looked terrified."

"Maybe he wasn't looking at you."

One of the CSI team plodded up the embankment holding a bag and called out to Marco. "We found part of his phone. It's in a million pieces and no wallet. But we can ID him with this."

She held up a sealed plastic bag holding a mutilated hand, severed above the wrist.

CHAPTER 13

Chronic insomnia was a bitch. Gabe spent the night waking from images of his copter crash spliced with nightmare flashbacks of Bobby running into the oncoming train. He gave up trying to sleep an hour before dawn when the mockingbird in the willow over his patio began its daily monologue. He swung out of bed, threw on a pair of shorts and a tee, and padded down the hall to the kitchen to put on coffee. While it was brewing, he checked his phone for messages. He'd called Tip when he got home last night to tell him about Bobby's death. Tip's calm voice eased Gabe's pain. Tip made an immediate empathic connection between Bobby's death and the soldier Gabe couldn't save. He had speculated that Bobby's second journey with Shakti had deepened his psychosis. No sane person would run into a train.

"My head is spinning, Tip. Nothing is clear. I feel responsible for Bobby's death, even though I know I'm not. I think a Journey would help me understand my feelings."

"Sounds like an excellent idea," Tip had agreed. "We'd best to do it while this trauma is raw. Your place tomorrow night?" They'd settled on a time and Gabe felt relieved. They ended the call.

Gabe poured a cup of coffee and carried it to his gym in the garage. He pounded out three hard sets of weights and logged a half hour on his treadmill before coming in to shower and eat. The bloodstained shirt he'd worn last night was draped on a chair in the kitchen. What had happened? Why was Bobby running? Gabe had grabbed Bobby to reel him in and they brushed against each other. Which meant that Bobby was bleeding before Gabe got there. "I've got to get out of here!" were his final words. Who was he running from?

Gabe waded through the backlog of client emails on his computer and went out to the patio to work on his bonsai with the question burning in his mind. Some of the miniature trees were more than a hundred years old and each one carried the imprint of its previous stewards. He'd been introduced to the art of bonsai by his sensei at the Tiger Lotus Dojo. The unhurried trimming process
transported him to a place of stillness that gave him a break from his ruminations.

Marco called at ten-thirty. He sounded weary. "Hola, Wakeman, you're not going to believe this. We've got an ID on the dead man. The hand we found isn't Bobby Wyring's. The prints are a match for a guy named Neil Ruston who lived in San Clemente. The police up there have notified his wife and told her the Santa Linda Sheriff's Department is investigating his death as a possible homicide."

"You're shitting me, Marco! I had him in my hands. I'd swear it was him."

"I can see why. I've seen their driver's license photos and they're dead ringers. Ruston was a landscape architect. Thirty-five years old, married, with two kids. We found his car parked in Seaside. Didn't you say Bobby was meeting somebody there? It could have been Ruston."

"He said he had to get away. If someone injured him, it would explain the blood on my shirt."

"We have several witnesses who saw him running."

"He was so scared he ignored the train warnings?"

"Maybe. It doesn't make sense. I'm going up to San Clemente to question Ruston's wife and I could use your eyes on this. You see things no one else notices. Do you have time to come along?"

"I wouldn't miss it. Maybe it'll help me find Bobby."

"I'll pick you up in an hour. Bring that shirt, I'll give it to forensics."

Gabe dressed and called Vince to tell him that Bobby was alive and explain the mix-up. He hung up and called Jessica Wyring to ask if Bobby had shown up. She was unexpectedly cordial and chatty. Bobby wasn't home, she warbled, but she'd be happy to give him a message when he returned. Gabe had been sure that Bobby was dead. Had he misread Jessica too?

Traffic on I-5 was light north of Pacifica. It was already hot and the bare hills of Camp Pendleton shimmered in the August sun. Marco unwrapped a power bar and offered one to Gabe, who shook his head. "Maureen says I need to lose weight. She's hormonal with the baby due so I'm trying to be sensitive."

"Boy or girl?"

"We'll know next week. I love them like crazy, but three's enough. *No mas.*"

"You're a good dad, Marco." Marco had been a raw kid nursing the loss of his beloved older brother to the drug gangs in Miami when he'd joined Gabe's unit. Marco's life could have gone the same way, but he'd chosen the military, and then the police academy. They'd learned to trust each other under fire.

51

Marco had shown fierce courage in tight situations and he'd become Gabe's right hand. Their partnership ended when Marco fell in love and decided to leave Special Forces. They'd lost track of each other and meeting again in Santa Linda made Gabe wonder if everything in life was ruled by fate.

The border control point was closed and they sailed into San Clemente. Neil Ruston's house was on the lattice of streets climbing the hills east of the freeway. The house was small and looked older than the others on the street. It had thick white stucco walls, a red tile roof, and a snippet of ocean view. The ironwork on the front door was coated with Rust-Oleum and the cement mixer standing on the walkway looked like it had become part of the landscaping. Marco stepped over a discarded masonry trowel and a bucket with a layer of dried grout hardened in the bottom and rang the doorbell. There were footsteps inside and the door scraped open.

"Mrs. Ruston? I'm Marco Brandt from the Santa Linda Sheriff's Department." He handed the woman in the doorway his card. "This is Gabriel Wakeman. He works with me. I know you've already talked to the local police and I'm sorry we have to bother you at a time like this, but we have some questions that may help us figure out what happened to your husband."

Justine Ruston didn't answer. She was a tall blonde with the patented good looks you expected in coastal Orange County. Her hair was uncombed and her eyelids were red from crying. She clutched a tissue and stared at both of them blankly as if speaking took too much mental effort. Gabe felt a wave of pity. She was trying to hold herself together and they'd come with painful questions. Justine nodded and they followed her down the dark hall to the small sunlit living room.

A stocky woman with assertively hennaed hair was seated on a chair by the open French doors. She stood and the force of her personality filled the room. Justine was a ghost beside this force of nature.

"I'm Louise Ruston, Neil's mother." She angled her wrist and offered the straight downturned fingers of her right hand to each of them. Her voice was husky with an inconsistent lisp and faintly British vowels. She had defined cheekbones and an apple chin. Gabe guessed she was in her mid-fifties, but today she looked a decade older. Thick make-up couldn't hide her sorrow or the blotchy freckles sun had splashed on her hands. She was wearing a black and white chiffon pantsuit with ruffled sleeves and legs that looked weirdly festive.

"Justine asked me to be here," Louise said. "I've lost my son and the sheriffs couldn't give us an explanation this morning. They said that he was killed by a train in Seaside, but they don't know why. I hope you can explain what happened?"

They sat and Justine collapsed onto a couch gripping a throw pillow to her stomach, letting her mother-in-law speak.

"Do either of you know why Neil was in Seaside last night?" Marco asked.

"I have no idea," Louise said.

"Maybe he had a date," Justine looked up from her pillow.

"You never miss a chance to put him down," Louise spat.

There was an arrangement of family photographs on the wall beside Gabe's chair. "Is this Neil?" he asked. The man flanked by two blond children in the pictures looked exactly like Bobby Wyring. Louise nodded.

"I was going to divorce him," Justine said. "He might have been meeting a woman in Seaside."

Louse shifted angrily and Gabe felt the tension between the two women. "He was a good father," Louise said. "He loved his kids and you had him sleeping on the couch. You needed to give him another chance."

"Another chance? He's been cheating on me since our honeymoon. He said he was sick of his life. Who isn't? What kind of a father does that to his family?"

"If you'd given Neil the love he needed he wouldn't have gone looking elsewhere!"

"He gambled away everything we had," Justine continued as if she hadn't spoken. "We couldn't finish our remodel because he kept betting bigger and losing more. He owed money to some ugly people. Maybe they killed him for it." Her voice didn't rise above a monotone.

"That's a terrible thing to say! You're slandering the father of your children."

Marco cut in. "Do you know who his bookie is?"

"I've heard him on the phone with a guy in Gardena. I don't know his name."

"Neil didn't owe anyone. I paid off his debts," Louise said.

Justine looked up sharply, but didn't comment.

"What about jealous husbands?" Marco asked her.

"He had lots of affairs. Maybe somebody's husband cared more than I did."

"If you think of anything, please give me a call." Marco aimed his phone at the family photos on the wall. "Is it all right with you if I take a picture of these?"

Justine shrugged. "Go ahead if you think it will help."

"How old are your kids?"

"Sarah is seven and Jeffrey is five. They're at the beach with the nanny."

"Did Neil have any male relatives?"

"He's an only child. He was planning to move back in with his mommy."

Marco pocketed his phone. "Do you live nearby, Mrs. Ruston?"

"I live above my dress shop, the Tattered Sequin, in downtown Laguna Beach. I've owned the building for years. Neil grew up there. It's his home."

"Where's Neil's father?"

"He died a long time ago."

"Did Neil ever mention a man named Bobby Wyring?" Marco asked.

Justine looked surprised. "I saw that name with a phone number on a sticky note in his office yesterday. Just a minute, I'll get it."

They heard her footsteps in the tiled hall and a loud crash. Justine returned with a yellow Post-it and handed it to Marco. "Sorry, about the racket. Neil's goddamn drum set takes up his whole office. I didn't give this to the police because I didn't think it was important. Who is he?"

Louise watched the exchange without expression. Her mouth was clamped in a narrow line and her body was unnaturally still. She'd be a good poker player, Gabe thought.

"What do you think?" Marco asked when they were on the freeway.

"Bobby and Neil look like brothers."

"I saw them in person and couldn't tell them apart."

"Neil had Bobby's number. Maybe they planned to meet in Seaside. But something went wrong."

"Justine was telling the truth about their remodel. The house is torn up and they haven't worked on it for a while. Lack of money or marital problems?"

"Neil gambled big and he was seeing other women."

"Jessica has the same complaints about Bobby."

"Interesting. But I think we can rule Justine out. If she killed anyone, it would be her mother-in-law. Those two women hate each other."

"Probably a reflection of Neil's manipulations. He was a mama's boy with a narcissistic personality who may have treated Justine like an object."

"Louise must have been pretty young when Neil was born."

"Hard to tell. She's had work done. She raised Neil by herself and hated to share him with another woman. I wish the children had been there so we could see how they all interact."

"She's a tough cookie. I'd hate to have her as my mother-in-law."

"I've noticed that yours lives in Miami."

Marco moved into the fast lane and grinned. "Did you catch how quiet Louise got when you asked Justine about Bobby Wyring. You think she recognized his name?"

"I'd like to talk with her alone and see what I can get."

"Have a go at it. Meanwhile we're no closer to finding out who Neil was running from. I'll make an appointment to see Jessica Wyring tomorrow. If you can come, I'd like you there."

CHAPTER 14

Marco dropped Gabe off at home, promising to pick him up the next morning to visit Jessica Wyring. Gabe collected the Santa Linda Times from his driveway and brought in his mail. His back hurt and he was hot, tired and no closer to finding out where Bobby had gone.

Had Neil come to Seaside to meet Bobby? Who was the intended victim? The strangest thing about the day was the resemblance between the two men. They looked enough alike to be brothers, but Neil was an only child and Bobby didn't have a brother. He felt the truth in his chest but the facts didn't fit.

Talking with Clare might help him. She refused to carry a cell phone so he called the TLT hoping Mac wouldn't pick up the phone and begin a rambling conversation. Sonny answered on the second ring and Gabe asked if Clare was there. "Just a minute." There was an interval of muffled voices and Sonny came back. "She says to come to her place at 7 PM."

Gabe thanked him and dug around in his refrigerator to see what he had to eat. Three bottles of Effable Ale, a jar of capers, and a carton of eggs kept company with a shriveled slice of pizza and a quart of clam chowder from the Green Market.

"What does this say about your life?" he asked the empty shelves. He stuffed the pizza into the disposal, poured the soup into a bowl, and stood in front of the microwave watching his solitary meal revolve.

He got Tip's voice mail and left a message telling him the dead man was not Bobby Wyring, but a look-alike named Neil Ruston from San Clemente. Gabe and Marco had visited his widow today and were going to see Bobby's wife tomorrow morning. He reconfirmed the Journey they'd scheduled.

Gabe scrolled through his messages. Jason De Veaux wanted to know if Bobby had shown up and joked that the intruder in the garden was an extra-terrestrial. Betty Lou Landry, another constant caller, wanted advice on her troubled relationship. Wes Keeler floated some alternative dates for his session. Gabe checked his calendar and confirmed a day. He sent a reminder to his Austin Group with the theme for their quarterly session in September. Cynthia Rayburn, who hosted Gabe's other Santa Linda Group, wanted Gabe to work with her troubled little sister. He called back. They talked for an hour and he scheduled a lunch with her.

Gabe was about to hit the shower when Vince called. His short-lived relief that Bobby was alive had been replaced by fury at Chad. He'd searched his apartment above the garage and found a meth pipe in the kitchen.

"I don't give a damn what Shelly says, that little bastard's going back to rehab or he can find another place to live!"

Gabe had helped the Conklins do an intervention with Chad last year. He'd ended up in residential treatment at an expensive facility in Colorado. "Vince, I'm really sorry. You're right to be angry but putting Chad into rehab without changing your family dynamics is doomed to fail. Shelly has to stop enabling him. I'm willing to talk with Chad alone and see if I can convince him to go back into treatment. If that doesn't work, I'll meet with you and Shelly on Thursday morning and we can decide your next step."

The street-side spaces at the TLT were full when Gabe arrived. He parked in the alley in back and walked up the path past Mac's repair shop to Clare's cottage. Sonny had wrapped the big oak above the fountain in fairy lights and they were beginning to glow in the waning summer light. Gabe tapped on the pane of cobalt glass in Clare's front door and she pulled it open. She was wearing a cotton caftan and had a towel in one hand. Her damp hair was drying in feathery wisps and her feet were bare.

"I've had a long day," she apologized, "Come in. I've been worried about you, Gabe. Sonny told me Bobby Wyring was killed." She motioned Gabe inside. The central room of Clare's cottage was shaped like an octagon. Doors on each side led to the kitchen and bedrooms. There was a polished burl table in front of the fireplace, two deep armchairs, and a small velvet sofa. Gabe sat down in one of the armchairs and Clare switched on a bronze floor lamp and curled up on the sofa. Gabe felt the shift in his consciousness that always occurred when he was in this room. Time paused and his senses opened.

"It wasn't Bobby. The guy who died was named Neil Ruston. I got close enough to grab him. He was bleeding and he jerked loose and ran in front of the train. It was horrible."

"Do you think you could have stopped him?"

"No, but I feel involved. Marco asked me to go to San Clemente with him to interview Neil's widow, Justine. Turns out she was planning to divorce him. His mother, Louise was there. She's quite a character. The two women were sniping at each another. Louise blames Justine for their marital problems. There were family photos on the wall. Neil and Bobby looked like brothers and Justine found a note in Neil's office with Bobby Wyring's name and phone number on it."

"Do you think they're related?"

"Could be. Bobby was adopted. He has an older sister but no brothers. Justine said Neil was an only child and Louise didn't refute it. I want to talk to her again without Justine there."

"Louise has secrets." Clare read his thoughts.

"She knows more than she's saying."

"Bobby's still missing?"

"Rudy Mayer knows a woman named Shakti in Pinecrest. Bobby came to a meeting at her house and plans to attend a Ritual there this Saturday. If he doesn't show up before that, I'll try to catch him there."

"You have a lot of clients clamoring for your attention, Gabe. Finding runaways isn't your business. What is it about Bobby?"

"I promised Vince I'd try to help him but I feel like I made things worse. His look-alike ran in front of a train. If Bobby was the intended victim he may still be in danger."

"Come on Gabe. Be honest with yourself."

Gabe shifted in his chair. "Tip says I'm lost in the hero archetype. In my family if a man can't right every situation, he's a failure. I know that sounds crazy, but I'm stuck with it. He's agreed to facilitate a Journey with me tomorrow night."

"People see the world through the framework of their own narrative, Gabe. If you are caught in a story, it is your own creation. You can change it."

CHAPTER 15

Gabe was sipping hot coffee from a travel mug on his front steps when Marco arrived to pick him up. His sleep had been shredded by stark images of Neil's body rag-dolling through space in the white light of the oncoming train. The weight of the train shook the ground under his feet. The engine roared toward Neil blasting its horn. The headlights converged on the track, trapping him in blinding light. Gabe was catapulted into the memory of his helicopter crash and the kid, Dakota, trapped in his seat, screaming at Gabe to shoot him as flames melted his face. He was relieved that he'd be seeing Tip soon.

The Wyrings lived on the inland side of Playa del Sur, the next beach town south of Seaside. Gabe and Marco stepped around a cement mixer and a pallet of tile in their driveway.

"You think Bobby and Neil have the same contractor?" Marco asked.

"Maybe remodeling runs in the family." Marco leaned on the doorbell and they heard the sound of hammering. Jessica had been angry, impatient, and chatty with Gabe on the phone. Who would she be today?

Chatty Jessica opened the door smiling. She was wearing tight black leggings and a matching sports bra. Her straight blonde hair was sleeked into a scrunchie. Even without makeup she was an eyeful.

"Detective Brandt? Please come in. And you are …" Her welcome included Gabe.

"Gabriel Wakeman. We've spoken on the phone. I've been looking for Bobby."

"Good luck. He hasn't bothered to call home since Friday," Jessica seemed unconcerned. "I told you I don't know anything about the man who was killed." She led them through the house to an airy kitchen overlooking a backyard strewn with toys. Gabe nudged Marco. There were framed family photos on the wall. Jessica with two tow-headed children and a man who could be Neil Ruston.

The granite counters in the kitchen were cluttered with piles of children's clothing and breakfast dishes and the hammering was coming through a door frame covered with plastic sheeting. "Sorry for the mess. We're adding a family room so the kids have a place to watch TV and Bobby can get his stupid drum set out of our guestroom. Coffee? I'm making a fresh pot for the carpenter." She waved them to bar stools at the counter.

The doorbell rang. "Excuse me. I'm not expecting anyone." Jessica made a graceful turn and left the room.

"Notice the photos?" Gabe asked.

"Duplicate families." Marco said.

"Bobby plays drums."

"And both of them gambled and had zipper problems," Marco said.

Women's voices blended with the hammering. Jessica returned looking irritated, followed by a petite brunette with sharp features and a sarcastic tilt at the corner of her mouth.

"Hello," she pushed by Jessica. "I'm Dana Wyring, Bobby's sister. I just stopped by to ask Jess if she'll take Mother to dialysis this Friday. Jess says you're with the sheriff's department."

She was wearing strappy heels so high she was standing on tiptoes, a thin silk blouse, and diamond studs. A delicate gold chain dropped into her cleavage like a directional arrow. An attractive woman who used sexual power to get what she wanted. Gabe knew Marco shared that thought.

"That's right, Ms. Wyring. I'm investigating the death of a man who was hit by a train in Seaside on Sunday night."

"What does this have to do with Jess? Where's Bobby?"

"Not that you'd care, but he's been missing since Friday," Jessica snapped. "Detective Brandt says the man who died looked like Bobby."

"Like Bobby?" Dana said.

"His name was Neil Ruston and he lived in San Clemente," Marco replied. "He had Bobby's phone number. Did either of you know him?"

Gabe watched the women's faces. Born mean, Bobby had said of Dana. He felt an instinctive dislike of her.

"I've never heard of him." Jessica said.

"Nor I," Dana's intonation was flat. Her dark eyes darted from Gabe to Marco.

"Maybe he's a business contact. Bobby knows a lot of people." Jessica said.

"Maybe he's the husband of one of Bobby's girlfriends," Dana was smug. "I told you I saw him having lunch..."

"And maybe you should mind your *own* damn business." Jessica glared at her.

The hammering ceased and the plastic sheet rustled. A hard-bodied man with tattooed arms who looked like he'd walked off the cover of a romance novel brushed the sheeting aside. "That coffee ready?" He pulled the hem of his T-shirt out of his jeans to wipe the sweat from his face. The fabric stretched against the pack of Marlboros rolled in his sleeve. "Hiya all."

"This is Jack Harrar, one of Vince's men. He's building our addition," Jessica said. There were two mugs beside the coffeemaker. Jessica filled one and handed it to Harrar. Their hands touched and faint color reddened her cheeks.

Harrar gave Dana a fleeting smile, grabbed his mug, and ducked back through the curtain.

"Neil Ruston was injured and running from someone when the train hit him. We don't know if his death was an accident or a murder. Ruston and Bobby looked enough alike to be mistaken for one another. Bobby doesn't have a brother, does he?"

Both women looked blank at the question. Dana shook her head. "He was adopted," Jessica said.

"The point is, Bobby, may be in danger," Marco said. "I need to find him. Could he be at his mother's?"

"No. I'm there almost every day," Dana said. "Bobby only shows up when he wants money."

"I'd like to talk with Mrs. Wyring," Marco said.

"Mother has end stage renal failure and goes to dialysis three times a week. She's free tomorrow morning if you come around ten."

Gabe and Marco agreed to interview Mildred Wyring the following day. They still didn't know why Neil was running or why he had Bobby's phone number. Both families were dysfunctional and Bobby's sister, Dana, was as snarky as their interchangeable blonde wives. Jessica had flushed when her hand touched Harrar's. Was something going on between them?

CHAPTER 16

Marco dropped Gabe at home. He downed a protein drink while he was standing by the kitchen sink and went out on the patio to call Chad. He answered on the fifth ring sounding drowsy. Clearly, he hadn't gone to work today.

"Wha'…"

"This is Gabe Wakeman, your dad asked me to call. I wonder if we could talk today? I can come by if it's okay."

"Yeah, I guess so. Let's get it over with. The old man never gets off my case, so you might as well."

"I'll be there in an hour." Gabe imagined reaching through the phone and slapping the selfish little bastard. He smiled at his fantasy. Chad's attitude had triggered his rage at failing to stop Neil's death.

Chad had been living in the apartment above Vince and Shelly's garage since his return from rehab last year. He was working on one of his father's jobsites and from Vince's reports, had seemed to be getting his life together. There was no answer when Gabe knocked. He rapped again and waited. He heard a girl's voice yell "shit", followed by giggling.

"Yeah, hang on a fucking minute," Chad fumbled the latch open to let Gabe in and stumbled back to his bed. A girl in an oversized T-shirt ran into the bathroom and slammed the door behind her. The small apartment was a mess. The air reeked of weed. Undone dishes and dirty clothes were tossed on every surface. Gabe cleared a chair and sat. He'd hoped that Chad would clean up his act after his last rehab. That didn't seem to be happening.

"I didn't realize you had company. I'm sorry to intrude, Chad. Is that the girl I met at the Surf Fair?"

"Yeah. Hayley."

"Are you two living together?" A toilet flushed and Gabe heard the shower come on."

"Friends with benefits is all. It's okay to talk, she can't hear."

"Your parents are concerned about you. Your dad thinks you're using again."

"They worry too much. I'm doing fine."

"Have you been going to NA meetings?

"I don't need to. My urine's clean."

"Your dad found a meth pipe.

"Jezus! He's always spying on me. That's the trouble with living here!"

"*Are* you using?"

"It was an old pipe. I found it in my sock drawer. My dad just doesn't get me. He expects me to live up to his stupid expectations. Both of them – even my mother - keep comparing me to my dorky sister who gets straight A's, and wouldn't know a joint if she saw one."

"You aren't at work today."

"Damn right! They say I either have to go to school or work, but why should I? I was never good at school and our family has plenty of money. If Vince wasn't so fucking tight, I wouldn't ever have to work. He gives me shitty jobs – even though I'm his son. I ought to be in line to run the company - he compares me to Bobby, but he doesn't make *him* do shit."

"Chad, these things aren't going to change unless you man up. Why don't we get a witnessed urine test and put your dad's doubts to rest?"

"You're just like him! You don't fucking trust me. You can tell my fucking father I'm not doin' any more drug tests. Now get the hell out and let me sleep!"

Gabe left the Conklin's feeling frustrated. They were going to have to plan another intervention, but unless Chad was motivated to change they were wasting their time.

CHAPTER 17

Gabe looked at his watch. Sam was late. The TLT's dinner crowd was thinning out. Mac and his cronies Big Wave O'Shea and Duke the Cabbie were hunched over one end of the bar debating the merits of artificial intelligence. Big Wave was a salt bleached blond giant who had traded investment banking for surfing. Duke was a Navy vet with the physique of a jockey who operated a one-man cab service in Seaside. He nurtured a passionate belief in a government cover-up of UFO's and panned for gold in the Rockies when the fever gripped him.

Mom was delivering slices of homemade pie and an admonition about manners to a table of unruly campers. They fell into line without a murmur of protest. Gabe smiled. Resistance was futile where Mom was concerned. She picked up the orange handled pot of decaf on her way to Gabe's table. "I didn't see you at dinner," she refilled his cup.

"I grabbed a sandwich after I ran," he fibbed. He was fasting for his Journey with Tip. "I have an appointment with Sam Gresham — she's in one of my Groups."

"Oh, *an appointment.* Blue dress, dark hair, very pretty? I think she just came in. I'll bring another cup." Mom smiled sweetly and bustled off.

"Sorry I'm late, Sam slid into the chair across from Gabe. "Matilda the Pug went into labor and had complications."

"No problem. It's good to see you."

"You too." She looked at the circling ceiling fans and the trio at the bar. Anywhere but at Gabe. The moment stretched between them. "This is a nice place." She brushed a strand of hair from her forehead and laughed lightly.

Gabe saw Mom bearing down on them with her eyes on Sam. She plunked a cup on the table and brandished twin carafes. "Coffee? Decaf? We have fresh blueberry pie." He knew she was dying to ask Sam questions.

"Thanks. Just decaf, black, please." They waited until Mom left.

"I'm glad you called. Is this about your last Journey?"

"In a way. I called because I want to get to know you better." Sam's gaze met his.

He was surprised at her directness and he liked it. She was beautiful, and that made him cautious. He reminded himself that she was still involved with her ex-husband. "I'm flattered. What would you like to know?"

"How did you become a shaman?"

Gabe reacted inwardly to her choice of words. Tip would say you didn't *become* a shaman, being a shaman was a gift you were born with. Or cursed with.
Tip had recognized Gabe's talents and taught him to trust his insights. He was still learning. He would always be learning. "I had PTSD after the service. Therapy didn't help and I found my way to Doctor Joseph Tipton. Tip saved me with Journeywork and I apprenticed under him."

"Then you began working on your own?"

"Yes, gradually." He didn't like to talk about himself and shifted the conversation to her. "How did you decide to become a vet?"

"I grew up with animals. They're easier to understand than people. I was an only child and my parents moved all over South America — my father is a forestry expert and my mom's a doctor. They're wonderful people, but they're absorbed in their work. They sent me up here to college at UC Davis and I got my DVM there."

"You seem comfortable with independence."

"I'm used to being on my own. Where did you grow up?"

"Arlington. My father was a West Pointer. He was gone most of the time. My mom is an artist and I have a younger sister, Sarah. After I graduated from Georgetown, I joined the Army like my father." Gabe reflected on the reality of his childhood. His dad's harshness, his mother's aloofness. "How did you come to move to Santa Linda?" he asked Sam.

"My ex-husband, Javier, is a war photographer. His family lives in Santiago. They're wealthy and he's never had to be practical. When our son, Rafi, was born, Javier agreed to stop risking his life for his next photo. There was a veterinary practice for sale in Playa del Sur, so we moved here. But Javier couldn't give up his addiction to danger. Three months later he flew to Syria and I filed for divorce." The words brought heat to Sam's cheeks. She aligned her spoon with the edge of her napkin.

"Have you ever been married?" she asked.

"I came close once, but it didn't work out." He'd fallen in love in college but their careers had taken them in different directions, and she'd died doing humanitarian work in West Africa. Losing her was a heartbreak he hadn't admitted to anyone except Tip, and more recently Clare. "Tell me about your clinic."

"Small Friends is more than a full-time job, even with two techs and another vet on staff. We treat dogs, cats, and the occasional rodent." Sam leaned closer to him. "I love my work- but I wish I had more time with Rafi."

"How old is he?"

"Six. I bought a house on the east side of Pinos Riscos because of the school district. My housekeeper, Alicia, has lived with us since Raft was born. With me working, that helps give him stability."

"And for fun?"

"The gym. Yoga. I coach Rafi's soccer team and we take Woof to Dog Beach. What's your life like?"

"I work a lot, too. Three of my Groups are out of town so that means lots of travel, and I do private sessions at home. My house is up the hill from here."

"I mean for fun." She touched his arm.

"When the phone isn't ringing, I manicure my bonsai trees as a kind of meditation. I run on the beach and I practice mixed martial arts with my friend, Marco."

"You sound as busy as I am. Do you stop to eat?"

"I usually come here to eat, but I know how to cook."

"Is that an invitation?" She was laughing, but her eyes were serious.

"How about dinner at my house on Friday?"

CHAPTER 18

Night was falling. Gabe had left the door to the outside
deck open and
turned on soft lights above the open futon on his living room
floor. His phone was turned off and he'd removed his watch.
Gabe had cued up six hours of ambient music.

Tip set the glass of ayahuasca he'd mixed on the table
beside Gabe and made himself comfortable in his chair. "After
we settled on your Journey tonight I had a long meditation. I
wanted my heart as open as possible to receive you. What do
you want to ask of the vine?"

"I need clarity. My rage about Neil Ruston's death has
got my compass spinning, Tip. Chad Conklin really set me off
today. I found myself wanting to strangle him because of his
attitude. I *know* that Chad isn't the problem."

"I know your story, Gabe. You are a good man who can't
always save people, no matter how hard you try. Your rage is a
defense against your shame. Neil died, just like your young
lieutenant. Neither death was your fault. You're haunted with
the horror of both deaths because you're bargaining with your
own grief. You're attracted to people who activate this dynamic,

72

and it will continue to haunt you until you befriend the feelings that drive it."

Tip touched the medicine glass to his forehead with respect and offered it to Gabe. "Drink up, my friend. May the power of the vine bring you the answers you want tonight."

Gabe drank the mixture and laid back on the futon, waiting for the familiar buzzing sensation on his skin to begin. Bamboo rustling beyond the open door to the deck started looking unnaturally green and the air in the room filled with almost palpable color. He closed his eyes, drifting in his visions.

Brilliant fractal patterns held his inward gaze in syncopation with his heartbeat. He felt himself spinning in space, drifting into endless darkness. A great cavern opened and there was an ancient priest praying over him, holding an obsidian blade above his bare chest. He couldn't move. He couldn't breathe. He fought the panic with surrender. His heart exploded into a thousand shimmering crystal shards that reformed into jeweled kaleidoscopes. Time lost all meaning as he slipped into the velvet eternity of nothingness.

The music played on, molding the shape of existence to the shifting colors of the room. "Are you coming back?" Tip asked. Several hours had passed. Tip sat at Gabe's side with his eyes closed, anchoring him to reality as they traveled into the realm of spirit.

Gabe was crawling through a relentless gauntlet of demons. They refused to let him free unless he counted them. *Three. Four. Five.* Numbers were vitally important. *Remember the numbers.* The vine spoke to him. *Three. Four. Five.*

CHAPTER 19

"Let's wait for Mother in the sun room." Dana Wyring led them through a series of dim formal rooms to the broad glassed-in terrace of Mildred Wyring's Mission Point mansion. Expensive holes ripped in Dana's designer top offered deliberate glimpses of creamy skin and her denim leggings were loyal to her curves. She had beautiful features and the description pocket Venus fit, but her seductiveness had an hostile undercurrent that made Gabe wary.

"Janie is still doing mother's make-up. She likes to make an entrance. Please sit down. Can I offer you something to drink while you wait? Coffee?"

"That'd be good." Marco took a seat in a padded wicker chair and Gabe took another.

"I'll have Janie bring a tray."

"This is quite a view," Gabe said. "Did you and Bobby grow up here?" The Cabrillo Bridge etched a graceful arc over Santa Linda Harbor. Pleasure boats bobbed in the marina at the foot of the hill. A hulking gray aircraft carrier was anchored at the naval base and sunlight glittered on a white cruise ship docked at the B-Street Pier. A view of privilege.

"Yes. We had a wonderful childhood. Our parents belonged to the yacht club and we learned to sail in the Bay. We both lived at home until college. Bobby went to State so that he could surf, but my grades were better and I was accepted at Vassar. I met my husband on the Cape when I was on a sailing vacation with classmates. We got married in New York but we settled in Chevy Chase after he started his company. You've heard of Bennington Biopharma? We had a branch in Singapore and another in London. I was dividing my time between continents while Bobby was learning the ropes at Wyring Construction."

"But you're living here full-time now." Marco stated.

"I moved back to Santa Linda because Mother's losing it and someone has to oversee her dialysis. Bobby's her favorite, but he never does anything. I'm the one dealing with her doctors and medical appointments. That gold digger he married is no help. Bobby's skipped out and Jessica's playing around behind his back."

"What makes you think she's cheating on him?" Marco asked.

"She's changed her hair color and instead of ragging on Bobby about not helping her enough, she's taking advantage of his being gone."

"Are you saying she has a lover?

"She's not home much lately and I saw her having dinner with a guy in the Gaslamp last week. They looked very cosy."

The sunroom doors opened soundlessly and a plump middle-aged woman in a pale blue nurse's uniform and thick crepe-soled shoes pushed Mildred Wyring's wheelchair onto the terrace. She set the brakes without looking at them and tucked Mildred's lap robe around her even though it was a warm day. Gabe and Marco rose.

"Please bring coffee for these gentlemen, Janie." Dana dismissed the maid and raised her voice. "Mother, these are the policemen you spoke to on the phone."

Mildred Wyring possessed a sort of brittle dignity. Cosmetic surgery had fixed her face in a rictus of permanent surprise and her hair was lacquered into a coal black cap so sleek it looked like a wig.

"Which one of you is Marco Brandt?" Mildred demanded.

"I'm Detective Brandt and this is Gabriel Wakeman." Marco introduced Gabe without explanation. "We're trying to locate your son in connection to the death of a man who was hit by a train in Seaside last Sunday. The victim's name was Neil Ruston."

"Dana," Mildred fluttered scarlet fingernails at her, certain of compliance, "please go help Janie make me a pot of tea while I talk to these gentlemen."

"Of course, Mother," Dana's parting acquiescence was candy coated.

"I've been supporting that girl since her divorce." Mildred stared at her departing back. "Dana's husband sold his biotech company for forty-seven million dollars but my idiot daughter signed a prenup and didn't get any of it. He left her for his secretary and Dana got a car and condo. Now she pretends to help me with my medical concerns while she waits for me to die."

"She seems concerned about you," Gabe said. "Do she and Bobby both help you out?"

"Dana and Bobby have never gotten along the way a brother and sister should. She only cares about herself but my darling boy would do anything for me."

"Do you know where Bobby is, Mrs. Wyring? Jessica says he hasn't been home for three days."

"No. I'm sure he will call me. He needs time for himself. Jessica makes so many demands. What connection does this have to that man's death?" Mildred was icy.

"The victim had Bobby's name and phone number." Marco showed her a picture of Neil on his phone. "They look identical. Bobby says he was adopted. Does he have a twin?"

"He does not. This is none of your business, Mr. Brandt. No one outside of our immediate family knows that Bobby is adopted. It is a private matter."

"Can you tell us who arranged the adoption?"

"I told you this is a closed matter. If you compromise my family's privacy the sheriff's department will be facing a lawsuit."

"I apologize for the intrusion, Mrs. Wyring. We're trying to find out why Neil Ruston died. Witnesses said he was running from someone when he was hit by the train. He may have been mistaken for your son. Does Bobby have any enemies?"

Mildred's wooden face came to life with traces of her past beauty. She was incandescent with outrage. "Everyone loves him!"

Gabe was unimpressed by her display. Indignation was Mildred's go-to emotion. Probably her way of dealing with anxiety. She'd been unable to produce a son and heir in the era when that mattered. Her disgrace had made her keep Bobby's adoption a secret from the world. Mildred's idealization of him had fueled his grandiosity while Dana's self-worth had withered in the shadow of her mother's shame. No wonder she needed to seduce everyone.

"I understand, Mrs. Wyring, but we need to talk to your son for his own safety." Marco said.

"I'm not feeling well, Mr. Brandt. Were there any other questions?"

The terrace doors opened and an aroma of freshly brewed coffee preceded the jingling teacart Janie pushed across the threshold, but Gabe didn't think they'd be staying to drink it.

CHAPTER 20

Tip suggested they take a walk through the canyon below his house to integrate Gabe's Journey from the night before. The heat of the day had loosened its grip and the pines cast lengthening shadows across the trail.

"We've talked about this, Gabe." Tip planted his walking stick in the uneven path and pebbles crunched under his boots. Brittle creosote bush that had surrendered to summer scraped the bare skin on their shorts-clad legs and a lizard darted across the hot sand. "Anxiety disorders are chronic illnesses. The fact that you've worked through your symptoms doesn't render you bullet-proof. There's a parallel between not being able to save Bobby - I mean Neil - and your old PTSD. You couldn't save that kid who burned in your copter crash and his death is on your conscience. Neil ran in front of a train and there was nothing you could do. That's what sparked your flashbacks." Tip wiped sweat from his forehead with the back of his gloved hand and bent forward with his palms on his knees to catch his breath.

"You have a compulsive need to right what's wrong in the world, Gabe. Your identification with the hero archetype gets you into trouble. It's a defense against feeling. You automatically act like the hero without stopping to consider *why* you take this position. What are you afraid to feel?"

"Helpless." Gabe watched a lone hawk drift overhead. Was he destined to isolation? "Last night in Journeyspace I saw it clearly, but today it feels a million miles away," He trusted Tip not to press him further than he was ready to go.

"That's okay. Let it incubate. What else?"

"Just as I was coming out, the vine spoke to me. I heard her voice, Tip."

"What did she say?"

"I was surrounded by demons. They wouldn't let me pass. They demanded that I count them. The voice told me that numbers matter. Three. Four. Five."

"Any idea what that's about?

"None. But I suppose you'll tell me."

"You give me too much credit. That's for you to figure out."

"Sometimes I feel like The Karate Kid."

Tip grinned. "Let's talk about Bobby." The trail narrowed and Gabe fell in behind Tip. "You said he ran away after you chased the intruder in the garden. If he's still using crystal, he's probably paranoid."

"Marco and I visited Neil Ruston's widow – he's the man who was hit by the train. He had a note with Bobby's name and phone number on it. Marco and I went to see Jessica Wyring too. The similarity between the two men is bizarre. Both men are drummers, married to good-looking blondes. Gamblers, both remodeling their houses, and having affairs."

"You think they're twins?"

"Bobby's adopted. Neil's mother claims he's an only child."

"Identical twins carry the same genetic makeup and similar neurochemistry. Maybe these two have a dopamine regulation deficiency, manifesting in compulsions and addictions."

Tip stopped and felt for his pulse at his neck. "Shit. I'm having another run of a-fib. Wait a second." He massaged his right carotid artery in slow circles. "That's better," he began walking again, "but we should take the easy loop home. Aging is a series of accommodations, Gabe. I wonder how much more is in store."

The harsh *tshush* of the snake's rattle spooled into the dry air. Tip yelped and dropped to his knees in the sand. The baby rattler slithered away into the bushes. "Little fucker! God, that hurts!" Tip cursed. "I couldn't see him in the shadow!" Blood ran down his calf, soaking his sock.

"Hang on! Don't move and don't stand up!" Gabe whipped out his cell phone and punched in 911. "What should I do, Tip? Do you need a tourniquet?"

"No. It's better if it bleeds."

The 911 dispatcher came on the line. "I'm in Pinos Riscos State Park Extension on the upper Ellen Lowell Trail," Gabe said. "My friend was bitten by a rattlesnake. He's eighty-four and he takes medication for a-fib. He's conscious. About two minutes ago."

"Tell her it was a Southwestern Speckled Rattler," Tip ground out. "It was a baby and it may have unloaded a lot of venom."

Gabe relayed the information. "I can carry him down to the trailhead on Pinos Riscos Scenic Parkway. Can you find me on GPS? Good. Ten minutes." Gabe pocketed his phone.

"The hell you'll carry me! With your back? I can walk."

"Goddamnit, Tip! Cut the heroics. You're almost eighty-five years old. In five minutes, you'll have trouble crawling out of here."

"We've got to keep the bite below the level of my heart."

"Grab your stick and let me help you stand up on your good leg. I'll piggy back you down."

"Just a sec." Tip was pale, he struggled to plant his stick and vomited. His leg was swelling rapidly. There was a grapefruit-sized bulge with two oozing holes at the site of the bite. "Toes are getting numb."

"Give me the stick. Put your arms around my neck." Gabe crouched beside Tip and pulled his full weight onto his back. He steadied himself with the stick to heave them upright. Tip grunted and hung on. Gabe grabbed his legs, leaned forward, and plunged down the trail. The deep sand dragged at his feet and he was panting when they met the two EMTs who jogged up the trail with a stretcher to meet them. They started an IV in Tip's arm and made the ten-minute drive to Lowell Memorial with their siren screaming.

Mags arrived as the ER doc was marking Tip's leg with a black Sharpie. His face was numb and he was having trouble speaking.

"Cold," Tip managed.

"I know, Mags soothed. "More blankets are coming. Gabe's here. I'm here. They're taking care of you."

"His heart rate is up and we're monitoring him for atrial fibrillation. We had to order more antivenom," the ER doc said. "I've given him a muscle relaxant and something for the pain. See that red streak up his leg? We're watching to see how quickly it's moving."

By 1AM Tip was stable and they moved him to the ICU for observation. Mags went upstairs with him and Gabe Ubered back to his car and drove home. He spent a restless night dreaming of snakes and woke up exhausted.

CHAPTER 21

Gabe showered and texted Vince to report that he'd gotten nowhere with Chad. He explained what had happened to Tip and rescheduled their meeting to plan an intervention for Chad. The phone rang as he completed the text. Marco was excited. He had reviewed a security camera recording from the Seaside Surf Fair.

"Neil was scuffling with a big man wearing a baseball cap that shaded his face. A few frames show what could be a knife or an ice pick in his hand. I'm waiting to see if the blood on your shirt matches Neil's DNA. I think Neil was stabbed and that's why he was running."

"The trespasser in Vince's garden fits that description."

"He could be the same guy. But we have no idea who he is or why he hurt Bobby."

"Listen, Marco, I've been at Lowell Memorial with Tip. We went for a walk in the canyon below his place and he was bitten by a rattlesnake. Paramedics rushed him to the ER, but he's pretty sick. They're keeping him in the ICU."

"Dios mio! Poor guy. How old is he anyway?"

"He's a young eighty-five, but he's got heart trouble and the snake venom is hitting him hard."

"Sorry, amigo, I know you care about him. He's like a father to you. Is there anything I can do?"

"Pray hard. And find Bobby Wyring. I'm going to see how Tip is doing and then I'm going to call Louise Ruston to schedule a meeting to shake the truth out of her. She knows more than she's told us."

The ICU was sterile, white, and impersonal. A lonely place to be sick. Gabe shut out the painful memories of his own long convalescence. Mags was standing next to Tip's bed feeding him ice chips with a plastic spoon. His leg was wrapped in snowy gauze stained crimson and yellow where blood and serum oozed from a nasty incision down the length of his calf.

"Compartment syndrome," Tip rasped. "It was so swollen they had to cut it open to allow blood return. I'll be okay. They're just keeping me here to monitor my heart."

"They should give you an honorary doctorate in denial. You can't feel your foot. You're woozy from hemolytic toxins and you're so nauseated you can't eat," Mags sounded exhausted. "The snake venom can make his blood coagulate and clog up his kidneys. His doctor is watching his labs for evidence of renal failure," Mags told Gabe. "She handed the spoon and cup of ice chips to Gabe. "See if you can get through to him."

"You should go home and get some rest, Mags. This is going to be a marathon."

"I don't want to leave him alone."

"That's my fault." Tip volunteered. "I've always told her how dangerous hospitals are."

"I'll stay with Tip. You've got to pace yourself."

"He's right, Mags. I will be fine."

She hesitated. "I'll be back in a few hours, Joseph. Call me if you need anything from home." She scooped up her purse, gave Gabe a hug, and slipped out the door.

"She worries too much, Gabe. She's a good woman and I'm lucky to have found her but around my health she's like a terrier on the hunt. Hell, I'm lucky to be alive. If I'd been hit by a rattler fifty years ago, they wouldn't have all this technology to revive me. Life is a gamble, son." Tip's voice faded like a cell phone losing its signal. "Speaking of gambling, I've been thinking about Bobby. Figure out where he goes to gamble and you'll find him."

Gabe watched Tip's chest rise and fall as he drifted into a fitful sleep.

He thought of his father's final days in hospice. His body was shutting down but his spirit refused to surrender. His last breath had left a hole in Gabe's heart that would never be filled. What would it be like to lose Tip? That cavern was too dark to enter.

He called Jessica Wyring twice but her phone rolled over to voicemail. Mags returned at three to sit with Tip and Gabe reassured her that he'd be fine. He promised her he'd be back in the morning.

CHAPTER 22

Jessica opened an IPA and set a plate with a beef sandwich on the breakfast bar in front of Harrar. She could hear the children squealing in the wading pool by the back steps. Jack's tee clung to his abs, his muscles were hard where Bobby's were going soft. She longed to reach across the strip of granite separating them and feel his body against hers, but the kids might come in. She and Jack hadn't had any time alone since last Sunday and the tension of having him around but not being able to touch him was getting to her.

"I heard your phone ring. Has Bobby checked in?"

"No, it was Vince's friend who was here with the sheriff. I didn't pick up."

"You think Bobby's still gambling?"

"Who cares? He does this. He goes on a run and saddles me with the kids. He'll drink too much and gamble too much, then come crying home to his mother to get more money so he can keep it going. When he's had his fill, he'll call me saying he's sorry and come crawling home."

"When will that be? I don't need any trouble."

"Don't worry sweetheart, he'll call first to see how angry I am. The kids are going to my parent's house tomorrow. We'll have the whole night together. I'm so sick of sneaking around, waiting for Bobby to show."

"It's just for now, babe. I told you. There's a guy in Seattle who's offered me the foreman's job on a huge project he's doing up there. It's a happening city. You could get modeling or TV work. You should be someplace where you're appreciated."

CHAPTER 23

Gabe was hungry but hospital food held no appeal and he headed to the TLT. Sonny and Chuy were in the kitchen and Mom was setting up tables for the dinner crowd. She put down the folded napkins she was carrying and greeted Gabe warmly. "Your favorite table is open, dear. Today's special is just the thing for you." Her snowy curls bobbed off to the kitchen.

Gabe tried Jessica's number again. This time she picked up. Her polite tone turned harsh when he asked about Bobby. "That bastard hasn't shown. I'm taking care of two kids and he's off somewhere with his slut. You want to know where he gambles? Try Three Feathers east of Pinecrest." She clicked off.

"Here you are Gabe, my Long-haul Lentil Soup." Mom placed a steaming bowl and a covered basket of warm bread in front of him. "You'll need your strength." She patted his shoulder.

Gabe was skeptical about Jessica's suggestion but he called Three Feathers and asked to speak with Bobby Wyring. He sat through an interlude of native flute music while he ate. A series of clicks. Bobby's voice came on the line. Gabe immediately hung up. If he left now, he might be able to catch

Bobby at the resort. "Mom, can you put this on my tab?" he called across the restaurant. He left a five on the table and waved goodbye to her on his way out the door.

He got on I-5 South and took I-8 East up the grade to Three Feathers Indian Casino. East of La Bolsa, massive boulders littered the rugged hillsides as if giants were playing marbles. Scrub and manzanita were losing a turf war to gated communities of mansionettes in dangerously fire prone country. Three Feathers Resort and Casino looked like a Disney Castle marooned in a sea of artificially green golf courses.

A chartered busload of Chinese gamblers crowded into the lobby, waiting to check in. Gabe finally reached the front of the line and asked the harried receptionist to ring Bobby's room. "I'm sorry, sir, but no one's answering."

"That's alright, thank you." An elevator pinged and the doors opened. Gabe looked up to see Bobby Wyring and a busty woman in an abbreviated sundress strolling toward the exit, giggling. A heavy-set man in a painter's jumpsuit emerged from the crowd. He crossed in front of Gabe and fell in behind the couple. The glaring heat hit Gabe's face like a blast furnace as he followed them outside.

Bobby and the woman went into the multilevel parking garage. The man in the jumpsuit trailed at a distance. Gabe hung back. He heard the echo of their footsteps on the concrete stairs two levels above him. A woman screamed. Gabe heard angry voices and sprinted up the stairs toward the commotion. Bobby and the woman were backed against a silver Sierra SUV with their hands in the air. The painter was brandishing a pistol and cursing at them.

"You cheating bitch! I've been following you and your fucking boyfriend! You thought I wouldn't catch you."

"Matt. Please. Put the gun down and we can talk this over."

"Fucking bullshit! He let out a string of profanities. "Step away from him Erin or I swear I'll kill you both."

"Listen Matt, I'm willing to just walk away and never see her again if that's what you want." Bobby started to lower his hands.

"Keep them up, asshole! I'm not done. I swear I'll shoot you!" Matt's hand was shaking. He sounded as frightened as the couple in front of him. Gabe figured he hadn't thought about what he was going to do next and that made him more dangerous. Gabe stepped behind Matt but Erin's eyes tracked his movement and Matt spun, aiming the gun at Gabe's face. Training took over and Gabe wrapped his left hand over Matt's wrist, forcing him to drop the weapon. The gun went off with a boom and scuttered away. Gabe drove Matt to the ground and immobilized his arms.

"Ow! That hurts! Let me go!" Matt yelled.

"Not until you calm down!" Gabe kept him pinned.

There was a shriek of tires as Bobby backed his truck out and reversed. Gabe saw Erin staring at him through the window as Bobby's silver Sierra tore past them.

"I was only using the fucking gun to scare him. I was going to beat him up and convince Erin to come back home. She's my wife! They've been having an affair."

"Were you in the garden at Vince Conklin's last Friday night?"

"I was tracking Bobby, but someone saw me. I hit him and ran."

"Did you follow Bobby to Seaside last Sunday?
"I was nowhere near Seaside! I have season tickets to the Friars
    and I
 was at the ballgame. My buddies will back me up."
Footsteps pounded up the stairs and two beefy tribal policemen descended on them with Tasers drawn.

CHAPTER 24

Erin was shaking. "I knew Matt would be mad but I never thought he'd pull a gun on us. That shithead! Who's that guy who grabbed him? Do you know him?" she asked Bobby.

"Gabe Wakeman. He's a friend of Vince's. He must have been following us just like Matt was. Perfect timing that he came along when he did, baby. My luck is holding."

"Where are we going now?"

"To my mother's house, just like before. I'm up twenty grand and I need more dough to bankroll this streak I'm on." He sure as hell wasn't going to go home. Jess would be pissed that he was on a casino run with Erin. But she'd get over it, same as always. When he threw a few hundred grand of winnings on the bed, she'd be real lovey-dovey. He'd never have to work again and they could travel the world with the kids. He'd always thought he was special, but when he was on meth, he could *feel* it.

After his psychedelic experience with Shakti he'd felt invincible and headed for Three Feathers to cash in. He'd called Erin to meet him there even though Matt had stalked him to Vince's garden. Erin was super hot and she was a fun diversion from Jessica's nagging. But if Matt showed up again, he'd cut her loose.

He'd blown off a meeting with a guy in Seaside on Sunday afternoon because work was no longer important—all that mattered was keeping this feeling going.

His next trip to Shakti's wasn't until Saturday. He'd been bumping a couple lines of crystal each day to maintain his high. The edges were crumbling and he was only sleeping three hours a night. He could feel himself coming down. A little less confident. A little less optimistic. He was running out of crystal. He needed to hook up with Chad soon.

The drive into Santa Linda was smooth at ninety miles an hour. They were in his mother's driveway by sunset. "Wait in the car while I talk to her," he told Erin. "Bringing you in wouldn't be cool."

Bobby unlocked the front door as quietly as a cat, hoping that Janie wouldn't hear him. He could count on her to cover for him, but he didn't want to listen to her whine about neglecting Mother. Mother's endless ailments were a drag and he was tired of hearing them. She'd have had dinner by now and be in her room watching *Downton Abbey* reruns.

He was padding down the carpeted hall toward Mother's room and he could have sworn he hadn't made a sound.

"Bobby? Is that you?"

Janie was there blocking the doorway just as she'd done when he was a wild teen-ager. She looked like an avenging angel in flip flops with a lumpy bathrobe belted around her waist. He'd always thought Janie would be half pretty if she'd lose some weight and do something with her hair. But she didn't seem to care anymore. His parents slept in separate bedrooms and he remembered his father slipping out of Janie's room at night years ago and not understanding what that meant. She'd been with the Wyring's as long as he could remember.

There was a woman who came in to clean and one who cooked, but Janie saw to their clothes and wiped up after them when they were sick. She drove Bobby to Cub Scouts and took Dana to piano lessons. When they grew up and went to college, she stayed on to become Mother's nurse.

"You've got me, Janie." He was her favorite and she could be charmed as easily as Mother.

"Bobby! What are you doing here at this hour? You're sneaking in after dark? What do you want?"

"C'mon, Janie."

"Are you here to ask for more money?"

"I know it's late, but if Mother knows I'm here she'll want to see me." Bobby's smile was confident.

"Dana and your mother got in a huge fight about her giving you ten thousand dollars to pay for your gambling. Your mother says it's her money and she can do what she likes and your sister got really mad."

"They fight all the time. It doesn't mean anything."

"This one was bad. Your mother told your sister she's going to change her will and leave everything to you. Dana screamed at her and slammed the door."

"Dana's a pain in the ass, Janie. She's hated me forever."

"Dana hates you because your mother and Mr. George wanted a boy. They adopted you and loved you more."

"I'm not here for a history lesson, Janie."

"You need to wake up and listen to me, Bobby. You'd better get a lawyer 'cause there's gonna be hell to pay when your mother dies." She grabbed his arm and held it. "There's something you don't know. You have a twin brother."

"What do you mean, a brother? I have a sister."

"No, you've got a twin brother, but Mother and Mr. George only wanted to adopt one boy. Two were too much to take care of. They let the other one go. The police were here yesterday asking if you have a twin. Dana asked me too, but I didn't tell her anything. She's a troublemaker."

"Keep it that way, Janie. I don't know why the cops were asking about twins. You can tell me all about it later, but right now I need to get a check from Mother. I'm on a roll and I've got to get back to the casino before my luck changes."

CHAPTER 25

It was after midnight by the time the Tribal Police verified Gabe's story with Marco and turned Matt over to the Santa Linda Sheriff's Department. Gabe was exhausted. He drove home and got a few hours of broken sleep before surrendering to his insomnia. He got up, dragged himself to the garage to work out, and answered a half dozen client emails. At six he called Vince to bring him up to date on his search for Bobby.

"Neither Matt or Bobby was in Seaside the night Neil Ruston died, but Neil and Bobby looked so much alike that Marco and I wonder if someone targeted the wrong man."

"That doesn't make sense," Vince replied. "Bobby doesn't have any enemies. You're looking in the wrong direction, Gabe. He's a good guy. I wish Chad were half the man he is."

At seven Gabe decided it was late enough to call Mags cell to check on Tip. She was at Lowell Memorial and about to go home for a shower and change of clothing. Tip's condition was unchanged, but he was grumpy and insisted that he was well enough to be discharged. Gabe was afraid he would be stubborn and sign out against medical advice.

Gabe was hungry and he wanted real food before his appointment with Louise Ruston in San Clemente at eleven. The TLT was humming with people who felt the same way. Clare stopped at his table long enough for him to order the special, but there was no time to talk. He called Jessica Wyring while he waited for his breakfast to arrive and asked if she'd heard from Bobby.

"Bobby called me last night." She was snarky Jessica today. "He says he just needs some space. I have the kids all week and do I get space? No! He's colossally selfish and he always has been! I told him the police showed me a photo of a man named Neil Ruston. He looked just like him." Jessica sounded indifferent about the likeness.

"Bobby was at the Three Feathers Casino like you said, but he took off before I could talk to him." Bobby evidently hadn't told Jessica that he had company. "He's going to a spiritual gathering in Pinecrest on Saturday night. "

"Spiritual! Is there a woman involved?"

"Shakti and her husband, Darin Red Deer, but it's not what you think - it's more like a New Age meditation retreat. I'm going to try to catch him there."

The Tattered Sequin occupied the ground floor of an aging double-story building on the west side of the Coast Highway in Laguna Beach's colorful business district. Gabe was impressed with the size of the store. Considering the price of beach area property in Southern California, she must be well-off or had bought the place before the real estate boom.

August was the tourist season. Curbside parking was impossible and Louise had told him to use one of the reserved spaces behind the shop. Gabe parked and climbed the weathered redwood stairs to the landing outside the covered deck that ran the length of the second floor. He knocked on the locked metal gate at the top. Damp towels hung over the west railing and a jumble of sandy beach shoes were piled underneath them. The deck was wide and the patio table, chairs, and outdoor grill looked well-used. Slatted metal blinds covered most of the sliding doors on the east wall.

"Just a minute!" Louise slid one of the doors aside and glided across the deck to unlock the gate. She was barefoot and one ankle sported a fine gold chain with a charm. The silky blue maxi dress she was wearing covered her shoulders and swirled around her calves when she walked. "I have to lock everything or some bloke will steal it," she explained."

"You've lived here a long time?"

"Since the seventies. I couldn't get along without an ocean view. Neil grew up here." Louise's smile slipped when she spoke his name.

"I can't begin to know how you feel. Losing your son must be devastating."

"You've no idea. I'm grateful to have had him as long as I did. And I have two grandchildren. I need to be here to stop Justine from ruining them. She's a self-centered bitch." Louise led Gabe to the patio table. "I'm going to get us some drinks. Iced tea okay?"

"That would be fine." Gabe settled into a chair, hoping that her animosity toward Justine would make her forthcoming about her son. "Without Neil to rely on, she must value your help."

"If she has the sense to accept it," Louise snorted. She went into the house and returned carrying an iced pitcher in one hand and two glasses in the other. She had strong hands with scarlet nails and the stones in her rings looked genuine.

"I called because Neil's death was not an accident." Gabe said. Louise set the glasses down hard and tea slopped on the table, but he pressed on. "The police have video showing a man attacking him. Neil was running away from him when he was killed. Do you have any idea who that could have been?"

"None." Louise sat down. "Bugger. He was targeted?"

"Justine said he gambled. Did he owe money?"

"Justine exaggerates everything. She blows more on clothes than Neil did gambling. He's gotten in deep a couple of times but I bailed him out."

"Could Justine have paid somebody to attack Neil?"

"I wouldn't put it past her. But I think she'd go after his wallet instead. They were headed for an ugly divorce."

"Your son had the phone number of a man named Bobby Wyring in his office. Neil and Bobby looked enough alike to be twins. If the attacker assaulted Neil by mistake, Bobby is still in danger."

"Neil is dead. Why should I care about Bobby Wyring?"

"Because I think you knew Bobby." Gabe watched her face carefully. "You're grieving something besides Neil." He was certain of his intuition. "Were they both your sons?"

"I don't know what you're talking about." The skin around Louise's eyes tightened. She looked toward the ocean and didn't answer.

"Bobby has been looking for you his whole life. He told me he's never felt like he belongs. I think that's what fuels his gambling and drug use. He needs you."

"It's not my business, Mr. Wakeman."

"What you know can stop another tragedy. Call me if you want to talk."

###

Gabe left hoping he'd pushed Louise into acknowledging the truth. He called Marco from his car.

"Hey Wakeman, I was going to text you earlier but I got jammed up."

"I'm on my way home from Laguna. I just talked to Louise Ruston. She's an odd duck."

"Yeah, I noticed. Did you make any headway?"

"There are so many similarities between Neil and Bobby, I think they're brothers. I tried to get her to admit that, but she stonewalled me."

"Our tech people say the DNA on your shirt is Neil Ruston's, which means he was bleeding before he ran into the train. There were three calls between Neil and Bobby on the day Neil died. We won't get the recordings for a few days. I really need to talk to Bobby to see what he knows."

"The man Neil scuffled with was big and dark. That description fits Matt Stimpson, but I don't think it was him. The gun he pulled was only for show, he wouldn't have knifed Bobby."

"We've questioned Matt and he was released on bail, but I'm not ready to rule him out."

"Bobby was at a Ritual in Pinecrest last Saturday and the woman who runs it thinks he'll be back tomorrow night. I'll call you if I find him."

CHAPTER 26

Gabe poured Sam a glass of chardonnay and went outside to baste the salmon he was grilling while she nosed around his living room examining the beach rocks and found objects on his bookshelves. Gabe had set the round wooden table on the patio. "Five more minutes," he called to her. He lit the thick beeswax candle in the center and went back inside for chilled salad plates. "Did you find anything you like?"

"I pick up rocks, too. Your bookshelves say a lot about you. Where did you get the pottery rain god?" She sat down at the table on the patio and kicked off her shoes.

"Colombia."

"I have one like it. We lived there for two years when I was a teenager."

"I was stationed there in the service." It wasn't a part of Gabe's life he wanted to remember. He took the fish off the grill and plated the food.

"This smells delicious." Sam raised her glass and he touched the rim of his glass to hers. "To knowing you better," she said. Candlelight painted chestnut highlights in her hair. Her thin summer dress exposed the lightly tanned skin on her shoulders. Gabe breathed in her presence.

They ate quietly. "You said you were a good cook and you are," Sam said. "Did you ever find out who was in Vince's garden the night of our Group?"

"Bobby Wyring was having an affair with a married woman. Her husband, Matt, was the guy in the garden. He was looking for Bobby because he wanted to scare him off. Bobby's been missing for a week. I caught up with him at Three Feathers. Matt was there and he pulled a gun on Bobby. I disarmed him, and the police arrested him."

"You disarmed him? You say that like, 'I bought some butter.' Does this sort of thing happen often?"

"Occasionally. I have quite a gun collection in my lost and found." Sam laughed and he refilled their glasses. "You were with Catharine and Diane at the Group. At Integration you said you were working on your feelings about your ex-husband."

"Holding Catharine was heart breaking. Her struggle with MS reminds me how short life is. My Journey last Friday showed me that Rafi and my work in the clinic matter. Hanging onto my relationship with Javier is a waste. I'm done with him."

"I'm glad to hear that. I don't want to complicate your decision."

"You aren't. I've given this a lot of thought." Sam finished the last of her salmon. She picked up her wine glass and collected her shoes. "Shall we have dessert inside?"

Gabe followed her into the kitchen. "I have lemon sorbet." He pulled the container from the freezer. She was standing next to him and the heat rising between them scrambled his thoughts. Dessert could wait. He shoved the sherbet back in the freezer and closed the door. The top of

Sam's head neatly tucked under his chin. He put his arm around her and kissed her. She didn't resist. They kissed again with growing heat.

Gabe's phone rang sharply with the tone he'd set for Mags and Tip. The sound shattered the mood. "It's about my friend, Tip," We were hiking in the canyon and he was bitten by a rattlesnake. He's in the hospital. Gabe put his hands on her shoulders to steady them both before he pulled away. "I have to take it."

"You do. I understand, I'll give you some privacy." Sam hugged him and went to the bathroom.

"Hi Mags, what's up?"

"Sorry to call you on a Friday night, Gabe, but Tip isn't doing well."

"What happened?"

"He's developed a reaction to the antivenom. His blood pressure dropped and his a-fib came back."

"I'm coming down."

"There's nothing you can do here, Gabe. I'll stay with him."

"Nonsense, Mags. You shouldn't be alone."

Sam returned with her car keys in her hand. "It's time for me to go," she whispered. "You're a good cook." She gave him a kiss on his cheek. "I hope your friend is okay."

CHAPTER 27

Louise looked at Bobby's darkened house. There was a
light showing from a back bedroom. She had found his home
address on the web and had come to Playa del Sur determined
to speak to him. Too many years had passed. It was time to peel
away decades of pretense and see what kind of relationship they
could have.

Louise stretched across an untidy stack of tile by the
front door and pressed the bell. There was music coming from
inside the house but no one came to the door. Before her nerve
faded, she rang again, leaning hard on the bell. She'd come too
far to give up. There was a walkway around the house and
Louise followed it toward the light she'd seen. Music was
spilling out of an open window. A man and woman were
making love on a rumpled bed. The woman was on her back,
her long legs spread, and blonde hair tangled around her head.
She looked a lot like Justine, but the man above her bore no
similarity to Neil. His powerful arms were tattooed and his hair
was black in the lamplight.

CHAPTER 28

"I wish it could always be like this." Jessica stretched a languid arm above her head.

Harrar ran his hand down her stomach and Jessica moaned lightly. "No hurry, babe." He'd miss having her hot for him. They'd met at a company party last year. Bobby was ignoring her. She was drunk. "We've got all night. Your kids aren't home."

"Let's make the most of it. That guy, Gabe Wakeman, called. Bobby is going to some bullshit spiritual meditation in Pinecrest on Saturday. He said he was going to try to catch him there and bring him home."

"You miss him?" Harrar kissed her breasts and moved lower.

Jack was irresistible, but she wasn't trading in her lifestyle for great sex with a day laborer. He kept telling her he had a deal in the works that promised big money. With Bobby out of the picture, she and Jack could move to Seattle and she'd get her career back on track.

"Not much," she held him by his hair. "I wish he was dead."

CHAPTER 29

Shelly and Vince arrived at eleven. Gabe ushered them into his living room to talk. Tip had looked like death last night. He pushed the image out of his mind so he could focus on the Conklins.

"I'm really sorry that I couldn't get anywhere with Chad."

"I appreciate you trying, Gabe. He's never been easy," Vince said.

"I hoped I could get him to listen to reason."

"We've been avoiding confronting him until we saw you, Gabe," Shelly was tearful.

"The meth pipe was the last straw. We have to get him back into rehab. He's using again, no matter what Shelly thinks."

"He promised he'd stay clean, Gabe, we've been checking his urine every week."

"You can't believe a word he says, Shelly. Were you standing in the bathroom when he peed? You know his little shit tricks. He pulled a switch and fooled us. He needs help."

Gabe knew this argument could go on for hours. "Look, Shelly, I know how much you love Chad and want him to succeed in life. But Vince is right, there's just too much evidence and too much history here to give him the benefit of the doubt. He's using, and you have to admit that or your effort to help him is going to fail."

"Listen to Gabe. That's what I've been saying," Vince said.

"You're never home to see what Chad's doing," Shelly protested. "He's going steady with a really nice girl now. They volunteered in my booth at the Surf Fair and she's helping him settle down. Hayley's parents are well-off, they live in La Caya."

"Your problem is, you want to believe him. She's probably working him for money," Vince scoffed. Shelly clutched a tissue to her nose and whined softly. She was still hiding from a lifetime of protecting Chad from the consequences of his decisions.

Gabe's phone rang. "Excuse me." He took the call to give Shelly a chance to absorb what he'd said.

"Mr. Wakeman? This is Louise Ruston. I'm in Playa del Sur. I came down to talk to Bobby, but he's not at home. Can you meet me somewhere?"

Gabe turned away from Vince and Shelly and stepped into the kitchen. "I'm glad you called, Louise." He damped the excitement he felt out of his reply. "I can meet you at the Lonesome Threesome Bar and Grill in Seaside – the next town north of you – at two."

Gabe took a deep breath and went back to the Conklins to see if he could nudge them out of their entrenched positions. His challenge was to get them to express their frustrations with each other instead of using Chad as a football. Vince's work-fed life had left Shelly lonely and resentful. Her alliance with Chad against Vince's authority emasculated him. It took an hour for Gabe to get them to see how their positions made it impossible for Chad to grow up. They agreed to schedule an intervention for Chad on Monday afternoon.

CHAPTER 30

Mac was perched on his favorite barstool reading a novel titled *Middlesex* when Gabe came into the TLT. He waved hello and Mac flapped a hand and pushed his horn-rimmed glasses up his nose in reply. One side was secured with silver duct tape and his bushy eyebrows needed trimming. Sonny and Chuy were banging pots in the kitchen and Mom was busy dispensing relationship advice to a young couple Gabe didn't know.

Louise Ruston had chosen a back booth. Gabe by-passed his usual table and sat down opposite her. She was wearing a dull green tee and wrinkled linen pants. There were crumpled napkins and an empty tea cup in front of her.

"Have you ordered? he asked.

"I asked the waiter to come back later." Louise's hennaed hair had lost its luster. "I walked down to the place where the train hit Neil. I don't know what I was expecting to find." She stared angrily at Gabe and her eyes brimmed. "Some trace of him in the dirt, maybe? Thirty-five years. For what?" Her husky voice was bitter.

There was no answer to her question. Sonny arrived with menus in his hand and Gabe shook his head. "Decaf for me, and more tea for Mrs. Ruston." Sonny intuited their need for privacy and left them alone.

They sat in silence. Louise fiddled with her teabag and set the cup down.

"You were right about Neil having a brother," she said. "I'm going to tell you a story. I've been carrying it alone too long and I need to share it." She waited for Gabe's nod.

"Between us," he agreed.

"I've never told this to anyone. I was born Ronald Ruston, and I spent the first twenty-seven years of my life trapped in a man's body. It's agony to pretend you're a man when you know you're a woman.

"Before the change, I was Slammer, the drummer for the British punk band, The Stash. We hit New York running and toured the whole US that summer. You can't imagine what it was like. Fans treated us like royalty. Sex, drugs, you name it. There were groupies at every concert who'd do anything with anybody.

"I picked up with a groupie in Pittsburgh and she followed us out to the Coast. She thought she was in love with me. They all did. The daft cow got pregnant and didn't tell me until it was too late to get an abortion. I gave her money and told her I didn't need the hassle of a baby and she split.

"It was a pivotal time for me. I quit the band after the tour and stayed in L.A. because I'd found a doctor who would give me the hormone injections I needed before I went to Bangkok for the chop. I'd yearned for this all my life. Becoming a woman meant cutting off contact with my mates. If the public got wind of my transition, I'd be splashed all over the bloody tabloids and never have a normal life. I had to go it alone."

Gabe felt the puzzle pieces lock into place but the moment was delicate and he was careful not to show any reaction that would stop her talking.

"While this is happening, this groupie calls me and insists she's gotta see me. She'd had twin boys and sold one to a wealthy couple in Santa Linda. She shows up at my digs carrying the other baby, looking really strung-out. She wanted money and says she can't take care of him. I believe it's true, and my hormones are kicking in. It's my chance to be a mother so I take him.

"Nobody knew us in Laguna. It was a good place to start a new life. I am a woman, and I'm also Neil and Bobby's father. It's bloody mind-bending."

It was. Femininity sat comfortably on Louise. Gabe searched her carefully made-up face for traces of Ronald Ruston and found none. What would it have been like to abandon your identity and become a creature misunderstood and condemned by society? Thirty-five years ago, transsexual was a four-letter word. The press would have crucified a celebrity seeking gender reassignment. Living a normal life would have been impossible.

"Do you ever miss being Slammer?"

"It's like missing one's childhood, Mr. Wakeman. You can reminisce all you want, but in the end, you have to move on."

"What happened to Neil's mother?"

"She moved back east. I heard she died of an overdose."

"Did Neil know any of this?"

"He had no idea. When he was ten, he wanted to know who his father was. I told him we'd lived together but it didn't work out and he died in a crash when Neil was a baby. Recently he'd begun asking about his father again. I think he may have

111

submitted DNA to one of the genetic testing sites on the Internet."

"Did you know he planned to meet Bobby in Seaside?"

"No. The first time I saw Bobby's name was on that Post It note from Neil's office. I went to Bobby's house tonight looking for him. Nobody answered the door. There was a light on and music playing in back. I walked around and looked through the window. His wife is a good-looking blonde?"

"Jessica. Yes."

"She was in bed with a big dark-haired man with lots of tattoos. It wasn't Bobby."

"Bobby's been on a binge." Gabe explained what had happened.

"Even if Bobby did something that resulted in Neil's death, he's still my son. Can I help you find him?"

"He's going to a gathering tonight in Alpine. He's been avoiding me, but he might talk to you."

"I'm willing to try. I'm staying at the Oceana Bed and Breakfast up the street. It isn't easy telling you this story. I need to be alone for a while. Text me when you're ready to go."

Louise gathered up her purse and sunglasses and slid out of the booth.

Gabe watched her make her way gracefully between tables to the front door of the TLT. He admired her composure. Her beloved son had met a horrifying death. In the midst of her sorrow she'd summoned the strength to help find his brother.

Gabe went through the kitchen and out the back door of the TLT to Clare's cottage. She was reading under the big oak tree. "Quiet morning?" he asked.

She placed a fallen leaf in her book as a marker and closed it. "I have the afternoon off and Sylvie and Marlowe are going to the Farmer's Market with Sonny. How is Dr. Tipton?"

Gabe dragged a chair next to hers. "Sicker. He's developed an allergic reaction to the antivenom and it set off his arrhythmia. He's still in critical condition."

"You're afraid of losing him."

"It's a bad bite and he's no spring chicken."

"Joseph Tipton pulled you out of the wreckage of the life you created to please your father. He helped you discover who you are. He's been more than a father to you."

Gabe studied his shoes. "I'm not ready to lose him."

"Grief is the cost of love, Gabe."

Clare watched the play of light in the leaves of the tree overhead. Neither of them spoke for a while. Everything *would* be all right.

"I had a Journey with Tip the night before he was bitten.' he told Claire. "I had a vision where I was counting my demons. I've been trying to understand if that related to Tip's bite."

"How so?"

Numbers mattered. Three. Four. Five."

"Did you find a connection?"

"No. I asked for the session to get some clarity.

"Maybe the counting has nothing to do with Tip. Seems like you've got an awful lot going on."

Gabe sighed. "The natives have been restless. Neil Ruston and Bobby *are* twins. Their biological mother was a groupie who sold Bobby to the Wyring's at birth and gave Neil to his father, Slammer, who was the drummer in the British punk band, The Slash. Slammer was in the middle of a gender change when the twins were born. He changed his name to Louise Ruston and raised Neil as his mother. She came down from Laguna Beach yesterday to meet Bobby. She went to his house and found Jessica in bed with a stranger."

"You are right about restless," Clare laughed. "Any idea who the man was?"

"Jessica had a carpenter working at their house who fits Louise's description. She's playing around. Maybe they wanted to get rid of Bobby and killed Neil by mistake."

"Where is Bobby?"

"Louise and I are going to intercept him at Shakti's Ritual in Alpine tonight. I want to convince him to come home and talk to Marco."

CHAPTER 31

Gabe's thoughts were scattered. Too many pieces in play. Tip ill, Bobby missing, and Sam … he guarded his feelings but he felt a surge of attraction when he thought of her. She had the power to break through his defenses. Was he ready to risk that? He climbed into his Rover without starting it, closed his eyes, and took deep breaths to release the tightness in his chest. He was backing out of the TLT to go to Lowell Memorial when Mags called.

"Please don't come, Gabe. Tip is finally resting. He's been hallucinating all day. He thought his hospital room was a jungle. It would have been funny if he weren't so ill. He kept referring to his delusions as 'damn distractions'. I'm going home to get some clothes and spend the night. Come up tomorrow."

"You're sure?"

"Gabe, I appreciate you looking after us. The doctors say he's stabilizing. I'll call you if something changes."

"I'll wait," he agreed in order to give Mags the space she needed but there was a pull of fear in his heart. He had an hour before he picked up Louise to head to Alpine. He drove home,

115

made a tuna sandwich, and ate it standing at his kitchen counter while he answered messages. Sam had left an ambiguous text: She'd had a wonderful time. She wanted to see him again soon … but wanted to take it slowly. *Women ….*

Urgent calls from clients had piled up. A celebrity chef in New York had asked her third husband to move out and needed advice. Another of his private clients was shooting on location in Vancouver and needed to reschedule his next session. Cynthia Rayburn's little sister had been hospitalized after an overdose.

Gabe dealt with the calls and texted Shakti to alert her that he was bringing Bobby's mother with him tonight. He locked the house and went to pick Louise up at the Oceana. She'd changed to a bright blue shirt and pants and brushed a spark into her hair.

"Ready for this?" Gabe asked.

"As I'll ever be," Louise's jaw was tight.

Her vibration was inaudible, but Gabe felt it like a high pitched sound behind his eyes. She was afraid. She and Bobby had never met. Now she had to tell him she was his mother. Would she tell him she was his father?

They caught the 52 East through the untended hills of Miramar Air Base, then 125 South, to I-8. A layer of summer smog presided over industrial La Bolsa; the rocks along the highway looked too hot to touch.

"Shakti is a body worker who hosts Saturday night Rituals open to anyone with $600," Gabe told Louise. "Her sessions are a mashup of Native American and New Age ideas. Her husband, Red Deer, helps her run them. My friend, Rudy, says they give people peyote and mushrooms; I don't know what else. Bobby's been tweaking crystal. He'll be attracted to the stuff Shakti and Darin are handing out."

"Do they know we're coming?"

"I talked to them this week and they'll cooperate with us getting him out of there. The last thing they want is trouble. We're going to intercept Bobby before their Ritual begins and try to convince him to come home. I'm counting on your presence being enough to persuade him."

"I wonder how much he'll look like Neil." Layered emotions crossed Louise's face and she sank into silence.

Gabe left the freeway at Pinecrest Boulevard. Shakti lived on a dirt road dwindling out of town toward a clump of exhausted looking pines that surrounded a batten board farmhouse with a drooping porch. Dusty sunflowers on either side of the wooden steps argued for optimism.

"That's Bobby's truck." Gabe pointed to a silver Sierra with tinted windows. Gabe pulled up next to it.

"What kind of people come to this?" Louise inquired. An Econoline with missing trim disgorged a bearded man in an Aussie hat and tie-dye shorts. His better half balanced a guitar case and a blow-up bed against the side of the van. He took them from her and they went inside. Dust blew past them; other cars were arriving.

"I'll leave the A/C on. If you'll wait here, I'll ask Shakti to bring Bobby out to meet us." Louise nodded and Gabe headed to the house.

Darin Red Deer was standing in the doorway dressed in tie-dyed parachute pants, cheerfully triaging people to the kitchen or living room. Some of the interior walls had been knocked out to create space for Shakti's exuberant oil paintings. Feathered dreamcatchers hung from the crossbeam and a shoulder mounted buffalo head glowered at the crowd in bewilderment.

"I'm Gabe Wakeman. We talked on the phone."

"Gabe, namaste, my brother." Darin threw his arms open. Strings of trade beads swung across his bare chest. "We're expecting you."

Gabe returned his hug. "Is Shakti handy? Bobby Wyring's mother is waiting in my car. I want to get Bobby out of here before the Ritual."

"No problemo. Bobby is way wired and we don't want any aggro vibes. Shakti gave him a cool down tea."

"She gave him herbs?"

"No, man, he was *really* wired. You can't trust homeopathic shit when the pedal's on the metal. She slipped him 10 mil out of her Valium stash to make sure he'd chill. It won't knock him out, but it will sure take the edge off. She took him out back to show him the sweat lodge. Go through the kitchen. You'll see them."

The kitchen counters were crammed with food and the industrial size refrigerator was accepting donations. Gabe squeezed past a zaftig woman in a muumuu and a yogi with a man-bun. The screen door sighed shut on his heels. The sweat lodge hunched near the back of the property. Old truck tires and squares of sod anchored rotting cowhides and strips of canvas to its bowed roof. A striking woman with long raven braids tied across her head and henna designs on her hands was seated next to Bobby on the edge of the empty fire ring strumming a lute. Chickens scratching in the dirt fled in mock alarm at Gabe's approach. So far, so good, he hoped he wasn't going to have any trouble getting Bobby to come with him.

Shakti stopped playing. "Welcome, friend of Rudy's. I felt your presence when you arrived."

Bobby looked up in surprise. His T-shirt and shorts were clean, but he looked frayed. "Hey, Gabe! Great to see you, man!" He hugged Gabe ebulliently. "I owe you for getting Matt off my butt. I'm sorry I haven't returned your calls. Like I told

Jess, I needed a little time off." His words slurred and his pupils were huge.

"You don't need to worry about Matt. He's been arrested for carrying a loaded gun. We need to talk. I know Neil Ruston called you before he died."

Shakti touched both men on the shoulder. "I'll be inside if you need me." She gathered her Indian cotton skirt in one hand, slung the woven lute strap over her shoulder and trailed back to the house.

"How did you know about him? He called me and said he had a development deal he wanted to discuss. We arranged to meet in Seaside but Matt was after me so I flaked. I heard it was a mess. Jess said he was hit by the train." Bobby swayed and wiped sweat from his forehead.

"I was there when it happened. He ran up to me in a panic and I thought he was you. Someone stabbed him. The police are trying to figure out who."

"Jess said he looked like me."

"He was your twin brother, Bobby."

"My brother?" Bobby's face froze in shock.

"Janie, our housekeeper told me I have a brother, but I …."

"Yes. And your mother is here. She's waiting in my car."

Bobby swallowed. "My *real* mother? She's here? Then the things I said about not belonging …." Bobby's voice trailed off.

"Are true. She wants to meet you. Come with me."

Gabe avoided the house and took the path that led to the front parking area. Bobby followed him looking stunned. Louise stepped out of Gabe's Rover when she saw them and stood in front of the car. Her hair shone fiercely red in the afternoon light. Enough power there to face this moment, Gabe thought. She opened her arms slightly.

"Is it true you're my mother?"

"You're Neil's twin. You look like him. You sound like him too." Louise had tears in her eyes.

"I knew I was adopted. I tried to imagine what you were like. Why did you give me up? You let the Wyring's adopt me but you kept Neil." Bobby's voice shifted to a higher register. "Who is my father? Didn't he want me?" The questions poured out of him. *The pain of loss disguised as interrogation.*

"Why don't you two take Bobby's car and follow me to my house?" Gabe said. "My friend, Marco Brandt is a sheriff's detective working on Neil's case. I'll ask him to meet us there. That'll give you time to talk." He wondered if she would tell Bobby her secret.

CHAPTER 32

Gabe called Marco on the way home to tell him he'd found Bobby Wyring. "Louise Ruston had a change of heart and she called me. She showed up in Seaside yesterday and couldn't find Bobby. Neil and Bobby were twins. She came with me to Pinecrest tonight to find him. They're on their way to my place now."

"That's great, Gabe. I can be at your house in half an hour. Keep him there."

Gabe checked his rearview mirror to be sure he could see Bobby's Sequoia. "When Louise went to Bobby's house looking for him, she found Jessica in bed with a tattooed man who fits the description of Jack Harrar, the carpenter she had working there."

"Which gives Jessica a motive for getting rid of Bobby. Lover goes after husband?"

"And knocks off Neil by mistake?"

###

Marco's gray Honda was parked in front of Gabe's house and he was pacing the driveway when Gabe arrived. He got out and joined him.

"Bobby better show," Marco was wearing sweats and worn sneakers. "I'm missing family night with the kids and Maureen's complaining I'm never home."

"They're right behind me. Meeting his mother let some air out of Bobby's balloon. He'll cooperate."

Bobby and Louise arrived on the heels of his words. Gabe made introductions and suggested they go into the house. They filed awkwardly into the living room. Louise chose a chair and Bobby sat down on the couch next to her. She looked drained; Bobby had clearly been grilling her on the drive down, and now he looked ready to fall asleep.

"You've been hard to find, Mr. Wyring." Marco said.

"I had to lay low because Matt Stimpson was torqued. I was having a little fling with his wife and he took it seriously."

"Where were you last Sunday afternoon?"

"Erin and I were hanging out at Three Feathers. I was supposed to meet Neil Ruston in Seaside about a development deal. I had no idea he was my brother, but with Matt on my tail, I couldn't show. Is he connected to Neil's death?"

"Mr. Stimpson isn't involved. He was with friends at the ball game. His alibi is solid. We've released him. He'll have to explain to a judge why he was pointing a gun at you."

"You're sure he'll leave me alone?"

"He's not your problem. But you and Ruston look alike and he was stabbed before he ran into the train. Someone wants one of you dead."

"I don't have any enemies. They must have been after Neil."

Gabe watched Louise's face. Would she tell Bobby she'd seen his wife in bed with another man? She flinched at the sound of Neil's name, but didn't speak.

"What about gambling debts? Did he owe money?"

"Nothing substantial and I always paid them off."

"Do you have anything to add to this?" Marco asked Louise.

She shook her head. "I told you no one wanted to hurt my Neil. This has been a long day, detective."

"Then I think we're done here. Don't disappear again Mr. Wyring, or I'll have you arrested. And watch your back."

CHAPTER 33

"Yo, Chad, can we meet?"

"What do you need?"

"An eight," Harrar said. "My house in a half hour?"

"If I'm driving to you there's a delivery fee."

"Sure whatever." Harrar tossed his phone on the bed and lit a cigarette. Important to keep it brief on the outside chance the cops were monitoring Chad's cell. Jessica was a maniac in bed with crystal and he wanted to keep her happy. She was legal and willing. He wasn't going down for another rape charge.

After the Army, he'd parlayed a series of grunt jobs in construction into a cushy spot as a security guard at a sprawling singles apartment complex in Playa Del Rey. All he had to do was wear a blue blazer, change a few lightbulbs, and lay sweet words on the tenants – half of them hungry, available women. He had the looks and a smooth line to go with them. Life was going his way until he flirted with an underage college student visiting her sister for the summer. She *looked* eighteen, but the little bitch changed her mind and screamed rape. He was convicted and did three years in Lancaster. He'd learned carpentry there and how to kill to stay alive; the world owed him for lost time.

Vince Conklin believed in second chances and hired ex-cons on his construction projects. Harrar knew how to schmooze. Convincing Conklin that he was a penitent aching for honest work was a cinch. He worked hard and kept his nose clean for the first six months. Once the boss trusts you, everybody does.

Bobby saw him as a buddy and hired him to work on a room addition at his home. Harrar was good at reading women. He saw speculation in the way Jessica looked at him, sex was a scent he gave off. Bobby was out having fun. She was neglected, bored, and dissatisfied. One nudge … He'd started tweaking when he was a security guard and continued in prison. Tumbling Jessica into bed took a week and meth turned her wild.

Chad was a puppy with access to high grade meth. Harrar had noticed him dealing to Bobby and some other guys on the jobsite, but he'd resisted approaching him until he was through probation and in tight. Harrar's tough ex-con persona and good looks were what Chad aspired to. A scratch behind the ears and a couple hundred a week and he'd do what he was asked.

Harrar showered, got a beer out of the fridge, and went into the half-furnished living room to watch TV. He left the corridor door ajar so he'd hear Chad arrive. The apartment was a dump: warped vertical blinds, scratched parquet floors, an area rug with a coffee stain in front of the couch and an upholstered armchair he'd picked up on the curb. Mismatched tables for his feet and the TV, but the place worked for now. His luck was changing.

CHAPTER 34

"Drink up. We gotta go. That was my man Harrar. I told him half an hour." Chad shoved the last of his burger in his mouth and wiped his fingers with a paper napkin.

"We're delivering to his house? Like, I thought we were going to catch a movie." Hayley deliberately dragged a lank fry through the puddle of catsup congealing on her paper tray. "You treat him like he's special."

"He's a good client, Hayley. I gotta take care of him."

"Does it have to be right now?"

"Jack makes it easier for me on the job."

Hayley pursed her lips into an impatient pout.

"It won't take long, sweetie. My dad is going to sing a new tune when he finds out you're pregnant. Bobby Wyring won't be the candy ass favorite anymore. Dad'll move me to management and my mom will make sure we get a new house. C'mon." Chad shoved his chair back and held his hand out for Hayley to slide out of the Formica booth. "Imagine, you'll be too big to fit in here in another six months."

"In your dreams," she muttered under her breath. She tugged her cutoffs down to cover her butt and followed Chad out to his truck. "Whyn't you ask your dad for a new truck while you're at it? This one has a blown speaker and the camper shell rattles." She snicked her seatbelt over her skimpy tank-top, lit a cigarette, and blew out a lungful of smoke.

"I just may do that. Smoking's not good for the baby."

"Like, you're the boss of me now?" Hayley gave him a dirty look and cracked open a window.

"When we get to Harrar's, I'll park. Wait in the truck while I go in."

"Why can't I go with you? If you'd introduce me to your clients, I could do some of the deliveries and we could double our profits."

"Too risky. I don't want you to get hurt. Especially now." Chad drove the length of the alley behind Harrar's apartment building and parked in a vacant space near the dumpsters. "I won't be long."

"Yeah, it's smelly here. Hurry up." *Bor-iing.* Hayley put up the window and checked her Instagram account. She'd missed a period, done a pee test, and made the mistake of telling Chad the result. Doofus thought she'd keep the baby. As if. She had no intention of fucking up her life with a kid. She only hooked up with Chad because he had the best stuff. He got his drugs from a dealer in LA. If she could get a line to his source she was out of here. Period. End of story.

Hayley yawned. She looked at the time and realized it had been fifteen minutes. Jesus, Chad. Was he going to take all night? He had the keys; she couldn't turn the radio on and she wanted a hit. She climbed out of the truck. The smell from the dumpsters made her gag. She grabbed her bag and retreated to the
retaining wall at the edge of the parking lot and fired up a joint.

CHAPTER 35

"Jack. I got what you need, brother." Chad poked his head around the door. The patchy fuzz on his upper lip looked like a creeping fungus.

Harrar stood and motioned him to the chair. "Want a beer? I've got Bud in the fridge."

"Bud's good." Chad flopped in the chair. He ran his fingers through his hair and dropped one leg over the arm.

Harrar ground his cigarette out in the overflowing ashtray on the table and went to the kitchen. He returned with a sweating can, tossed it to Chad, and took a seat on the couch. "Tell me what you've got for me."

"The best L.A. Glass. It'll keep you tickin'."

"How much?"

"Two-fifty for an 8-Ball. For you, I'll eat the delivery fee." Chad waved a baggie at him.

"This your usual?"

"No, man, this stuff is way better."

"Gimme a taste and if it's as good as you say, we have a deal."

Chad spread a thin line on the tabletop and chopped it with a credit card. He popped the cartridge out of a disposable pen and handed to Harrar, who leaned over and snorted. "Whuf." Harrar pinched the bridge of his nose with his fingers and shuddered. He reached in his shirt pocket and counted out bills on the table.

"Just one?" Chad scooped up the cash and handed Harrar a fresh baggie.

"Yeah, it's more than enough."

Chad cracked his beer and took a swig. "Hey, you still moonlighting at Wyring's? Must be a sweet job with Jessica home all day."

"The money's good."

"I saw you pat her on the butt at Bobby's birthday party last month. She didn't look too upset."

"So? It was a party." Harrar's tone was a warning.

"I just mean you got it going on, Jack."

"Let's leave it alone," Harrar's eyes narrowed.

"Dana Wyring has the hots for you too," Chad smirked.

"The fuck you mean?"

"You were grinding her into the hood of her Mercedes in the parking lot and she was loving it, man. It wasn't that dark."

"What I think is you should keep your nose out of where it doesn't belong."

"Hey, you got me all wrong, Jack. I'm saying, you're the man. Women wanta fuck you and you don't take shit from anybody. That's all. Like when you kicked Bobby's ass at the Surf Fair."

"What the fuck you talking about?" The rush was hitting, the stuff was stronger than he'd expected; his brain was burning but Chad's words registered.

"Your fight with Bobby. You totally dominated him. I saw him running away."

Harrar stood and lunged forward and grabbed the neck of Chad's T-shirt with both hands. "I said don't stick your nose where it doesn't belong, you little fucker!" The shirt ripped. He lifted Chad up and slammed him against the wall. "What does it take for you to get the fucking idea?" Fury blinded him. He smashed his forearm into Chad's face. The blow broke his nose and blood poured down his chest.

Chad tried to raise his arms but Harrar had him pinned. He flailed and Harrar landed a furious combination of blows to his torso. Ribs cracked and Chad collapsed on the floor whimpering. Harrar kicked him in the face with his boot and he stopped moving.

Harrar backed onto the couch arm to catch his wind. Chad was lying in a heap making gurgling sounds. Harrar lipped a cigarette, lit it, and inhaled deeply. Blood hammered in his ears. He picked up his phone. Two rings.

"Dana. Baby. We got a problem. Meet me outside your place in twenty minutes."

CHAPTER 36

Chad wasn't moving. His face was black with clotted blood. Harrar found another 8 in his pants pocket along with his phone, a Velcro wallet, disposable lighter, and truck keys. Harrar pushed the scarred coffee table aside. He dragged Chad's limp body onto the ratty area rug in front of the couch and rolled him like a burrito. He'd deal with the blood on the floor later.

He shoved Chad's things in his own pockets and went downstairs. Chad had parked his truck in a dimly lit visitor's slot near the dumpsters. Television explosions thumped through the windows of the condo next door, but he had the hollow canyon of the parking area to himself. He unlocked the camper shell and lowered the tailgate of Chad's pickup so it was ready to load and trotted back up to his apartment.

###

The squeak of Chad's tailgate falling open stopped Hayley mid-toke. She dropped her joint, stepped on it, and backed into the darkest shadow. The man opening Chad's truck was a stranger. *Jack Harrar?* It had to be. Chad had gone up to his apartment and hadn't come out.

Harrar heaved the carpet on his shoulder. The sagging roll was hard to balance and Chad's head smacked the apartment door on the way out. Harrar cursed. Sneaking a body into a pickup without being seen was only the first problem. Dana was going to go fucking ape shit.

The walkway was empty. Harrar made sure he was clear and humped the rolled rug across the pavement to Chad's truck.

Hayley's warm buzz flipped to paranoia. Her heart was pounding in her throat. She rummaged in her purse for her phone and called Chad; the pot she'd smoked made her fingers clumsy. Chad hadn't come back. A stranger had used his key to open the truck. The carpet was big enough to hold a man.

Harrar felt Chad's phone vibrate against his leg. He dumped the carpet on the tailgate and shoved it far enough in to close the shell. He pawed for the offending phone and held it up to see who was calling. 'Hayley' appeared on the lighted screen with the picture of a grinning blonde girl. His gaze traveled past the image to the half wall at the end of the parking area and stopped. The same girl crouched in the shadow, staring toward him. The light from her phone haloed her hair and the pale oval of her face.

Harrar didn't hesitate.

###

Hayley was already moving. She clambered up the short wall, ran along the concrete block edging, leapt over a swath of groundcover and dove into the profusion of unkempt plumbago bushes planted between the buildings. They scratched her. She was panting from the short sprint. There was no way she could outrun her pursuer. She heard him strike the bushes over her head, cursing and trying to dislodge the branches so that he could see the ground. His legs tangled in the mass. Brute force wasn't an advantage. Hayley was small, she could wiggle underneath. She tucked her purse under her body, pulled her hoodie over her hair, and clung to the ground imagining herself sinking into it. Her breath came in inaudible puffs like a frightened rabbit.

###

Harrar searched the length of the bushes and came out on the street above his building. He had to find her fast. Dana was waiting and they had to get rid of Chad's body. A car drove up the street; its headlights swept his knees and lit the walks between the apartment buildings. Searching for Chad's girlfriend in the dark was a fool's errand. She could have taken off in any direction.

He backtracked to his own building, swearing under his breath. Chad was a dead man the moment he talked about seeing him brace Bobby's double at the Surf Fair. He hadn't counted on having to deal with the fucking girlfriend. His truck was parked in the row of resident's carports. He grabbed a shovel from the back and carried it to Chad's truck.

###

Hayley heard Harrar's footsteps pass by her hiding place but she was too frightened to move. The surge of adrenalin that had propelled her into her hiding place faded and she became aware of rough dirt under her cheek and the stink of dog turds in her nose. Her bare arms stung and branches had snagged her hair. She heard the rattle of Chad's truck engine starting up. The rolled carpet had been big enough and heavy enough to hold a man. Chad. The father of her unborn child. She tried to inject some feeling into the thought and succeeded in squeezing out a wash of dramatic tears. She was practically his partner. What was his was hers. Once she got rid of Harrar. It was only right that she take over Chad's drug clients.

Chad's truck left and there was no sound from the parking lot behind Harrar's apartment building. Hayley crawled out of the hedge and walked upslope, away from the parking lot onto the parallel street. She noted the number stenciled on the curb and called an Uber. She had to find the stash Chad kept in his apartment before anyone looked there. She'd grab the money and go to her parent's house in La Caya, a low-life like Harrar wouldn't look for her there. She raked dead leaves from her hair and gnawed a nail while she waited.

CHAPTER 37

Traffic was typical for a Saturday night. Harrar looked for a gap in traffic and tossed Chad's phone out the window onto the slow lane of the 805 South. Its last location would show it heading south toward Mexico.

Dana was standing in the doorway of her condo with the entry light off when Harrar drove up. She didn't react, except to take a step toward her door, until he got out and waved.

"What are you doing in this?" Dana demanded. She jumped in beside him and ran her hand along his thigh.

"It's Chad Conklin's."

"You said we have a problem."

"Fucking right. Chad came over to sell me an 8-Ball tonight and started mouthing off about seeing us together in the parking lot at Bobby's birthday."

"So what? You did me on the hood of my car. You couldn't wait, as I remember."

"Listen to me goddamnit! Chad can tie us together!"

"If they can link us, we're in trouble." Dana pulled away from him as if he was contagious.

135

"I had to ice him. He saw me knife the guy I thought was Bobby at the Surf Fair. He can place me with him minutes before he ran into the train."

"Jesus, Jack! First you fuck up and stab the wrong guy and now you tell me you killed Chad? You're an idiot! What did you do with his body?"

"It's in back." Harrar drummed his fingers on the steering wheel. He figured this wasn't the time to tell her about the girlfriend.

"You're driving around with a dead body? Has the meth addled your brain?"

"We've got to get rid of it."

"How do you propose to do that?"

"He's rolled up in a carpet. We need somewhere to dump him."

"You're the criminal. What do you suggest?"

"There's a Crispy Chip distribution center in Buena Mesa that's deserted at night. I saw it when Vince sent me to pick up some windows for the job. There's a drainage ditch behind the warehouse. We can bury the body there and no one will find it for months."

"What about DNA?"

"Bleach will destroy it. Follow me in your car. We'll stop at a 7-11 on our way and pick up a gallon."

"You want *me* to go in and buy it? Those places have cameras."

"A woman buying laundry bleach? That's not unusual."

"Not this woman."

"This is your problem too."

"We wouldn't have a problem if you hadn't knifed the wrong man. Chad is your screw up!"

"Killing your brother was *your* fucking idea. How was I to know he had a double? I'm helping you get the money like you asked!"

"All right! Just … no more screwups." Dana took a deep breath. "I've put up with Mother's shit my whole life. I'm not going to lose the money now. If Bobby doesn't die before she does, he'll get everything."

"Come here, baby." Harrar pulled her close and tried to kiss her. "A few days and we're set. We're a pair, you and me. We think alike."

Dana pushed him away. "We have a body to get rid of."

The industrial area of Buena Mesa was eerily quiet at night. Widely spaced street lights reflected on sleeping rows of white delivery vans with the familiar red Crispy Chip logo on their sides. A warehouse was set at the far end of the lot with an oleander hedge planted behind it. Harrar backed along the side of the warehouse with the rear of the truck toward the hedge. Dana parked near him, and got out, gingerly carrying a jug of bleach. Harrar opened the camper shell and handed her a flashlight.

"Bring the bleach and keep the light pointed down." Harrar picked up the shovel and stepped into the darkness. The uneven ground was littered with crushed cans and windblown paper. He ducked under the tree branches and kicked apart the mesh of dead weeds at the edge of the field. Dana aimed the light at Harrar's feet. He jammed the shovel into the dirt. Oleander roots snaked in all directions. "Jesus fucking Christ," Harrar cursed under his breath.

"What's wrong?" Dana asked.

"These roots. We've gotta bury Chad here and hope nobody finds him. Can you please shine the fucking light where I'm digging?"

137

"Sorry, Jack." Dana aimed the light into the shallow trench while he dug.
"What happens next?"

"When I finish …this … hole … we go back and get Chad's body." Harrar kept digging. "That's enough." He stuck the shovel in the dirt.

"What about the bleach?"

"Leave it here, c'mon." Harrar led the way back to the truck. He lowered the tailgate and pulled the carpet to the edge.

"You could have warned me to wear sneakers." Dana leaned against the truck and poured dirt out of her shoe.

"Don't touch anything! You'll leave prints." Harrar took a deep breath. He hoisted the carpet on his shoulder and staggered back toward the trees with Dana following. He dropped the carpet on the ground beside the trench and gave it a kick. The carpet unrolled and Chad's bloodied face stared up at them.

"Ohmygod!"

The beam of the flashlight shot skyward. Harrar grabbed it and snapped it off. "Hold it down, for chrissakes and hand me the bleach." Harrar uncapped the bottle and splashed it over the body. "I've gotta get his backside too. Help me flip him."

"No way," Dana wrapped her arms around her body and turned away gagging. "He's your mistake."

"Goddamnit Dana, you could help."

"I'm not touching him, Jack."

Harrar shoved Chad's shoulder with his boot to turn him over. He emptied the rest of the bleach on him and began throwing dirt in the grave.

"What do we do about the rug and his truck?" Dana asked.

"We drop the carpet in a dumpster. We'll wipe the truck clean and leave it in Little Asia with the keys in the ignition. It won't be there long." Harrar finished shoveling and wiped sweat from his face.

"Let's get out of here and dump Chad's truck." Dana picked up the empty bleach bottle with the tips of her fingers. I want to go home and clean up. I'll drop you at your apartment so you can get your truck and come over to my place. We need a new plan to get rid of Bobby."

CHAPTER 38

Hayley had the Uber driver let her off at the foot of the Conklin's driveway. Their house was like a block from the street. She jogged the whole way and wobbled up the stairs. Chad had given her a key to his apartment. His laptop was on the table in the dinette. She unplugged it, looking for notes he might have scribbled and left on the table. It was too big to fit in her purse; she shook out a plastic bag from Von's Market and shoved the cords in with the laptop. He wasn't smart enough to encrypt the customer info inside, she'd suss out his password later. Right now, she had to hurry.

The light on the outside stairs snapped on. Hayley jumped like a scalded cat.

"Chad? Are you home, darling? I didn't hear your car." Shelly Conklin tapped on the screen door at the top of the stairs and walked in. "Vince is snoring in front of the TV, but I couldn't sleep."

"It's just me, Mrs. Conklin," Hayley slid the Von's bag under the table. Chad's mom had to come snooping around like they were still kids. Flowered pajama bottoms peeked out below her robe. Her face was pale without makeup, and Hayley could smell gin on her breath.

"Where's Chad?"

"We met up with some friends at the beach, and I got tired, so I Uber-ed home. He'll be along later." Hayley felt sweat break out along her hairline. Harrar could show up at any minute.

Shelly looked like she hoped she'd be invited to stay. Instead, Hayley yawned widely. "I have a job interview in the morning and I need to get some sleep."

"Oh," Shelly tightened the tie of her bathrobe around her waist. "I guess I'd better let you go, you want to be fresh for that. Give Chad a hug for me."

Hayley didn't wait for her disappointed footsteps to reach the bottom of the stairs before she lifted the framed poster of Kurt Cobain off the wall behind the couch. Chad had cut a square hole in the plaster between the studs. His stash was packed in labeled Ziploc bags. The cash was in envelopes. She dumped the lot into her purse without counting and re-hung the poster. Time was wasting. She grabbed the computer, called an Uber, and ran down the driveway to wait.

Harrar stopped his truck across the street from the gate and looked up the curving drive. Chad Conklin lived in an apartment above Vince's garage. With any luck he would catch Chad's little bitch girlfriend there and silence her for good. He didn't have time to spare. Dana was expecting him at her house. She'd go nuclear if she found out the girlfriend had seen him dumping Chad's body tonight and he hadn't told her.

Headlights lit up his back window and he ducked. A blue Prius with an Uber decal in the rear window pulled into the curb ahead of him and cut its lights. A small figure appeared, running hard down the driveway, and threw itself into the Prius. Harrar swore aloud. The fucking girlfriend.

The Prius reversed in the street and Harrar dropped below the dash as the headlights swept the cab of his truck. He gave them a long lead and followed them through the twisting residential streets to the Coast Highway. The Prius turned south toward La Caya and Harrar followed. The car stopped at a house off La Caya Boulevard and he watched as the girl thanked the driver and ran inside. He texted the address to his phone.

CHAPTER 39

Dana met him at the front entry of her condo in stiff silence. Harrar waited until they were inside before he put his arm around her.

"You've been gone forever. Where've you been?"

"C'mon baby, slow down. Whoa. I was making sure my apartment was clean. We've got all night to plan, right now I want you." Killing Chad and chasing his girlfriend through the bushes had left him vibrating with tension and he knew Dana felt the same excitement.

"I'm not used to this shit, Jack." She relented enough to soften in his arms. "You act like what we did tonight is normal."

"Make us a drink, babe." Harrar urged her into the open kitchen. The living room was unlit. A wall of windows looked out on the darkened city. Chad's girlfriend was still alive. If she was involved in his drug dealing she wouldn't go to the police. She was a threat Dana didn't need to know about.

"What were you thinking? You're a fucking idiot!" Dana opened the freezer door. She dumped ice cubes and vodka into two glasses and slammed them on the granite. "They're going to find Chad. They can use his phone to track him to your place."

"Relax, baby. I ditched his phone in the middle of the 805. It's in a thousand pieces by now."

"All I wanted to do was get Bobby out of the way. One simple task and you couldn't even do that. First you go and stab the wrong man. Next you kill Chad!" She picked up her glass and took a deep drink. "What kind of a partner are you?"

"This kind." Harrar put his arms around her. "We got something good going, baby."

"You stink, Jack," she wriggled out of his embrace.

"Don't worry, I'll take care of Bobby." He pulled his dirty shirt over his head and draped it over a stool. "Why don't you join me in the shower? "

Dana followed him to the bathroom. "You'd better hurry. I had another fight with Mother. She gave Bobby ten thousand to cover his losses at the casino and I blew up. She threatened to cut me out of the will completely."

He'd heard this rant before. "Are you coming in with me?" He turned on the shower and dropped his pants.

"I've spent a lifetime taking care of her, and I don't get any thanks. She takes me for granted. My father was the same. He didn't see me either. The business had to go to their precious Bobby. Neither of them ever considered that I could run it, even though I'm smarter. Mother is going to die soon and the Crowned Prince will get everything unless he dies first."

Harrar liked Dana when she was in this mood. Her anger translated into furious sex. The madder she was the hotter she'd be in bed.

Hours later, Harrar got up to go to the bathroom and discovered he was alone. Dana was sitting on the outside balcony smoking a cigarette.

144

"Babe?" He ruffled her hair. "Since when do you smoke?"

"When I have a brainstorm," her teeth glinted in the ambient light. "Do you know where Bobby is going to be tomorrow?"

"I can find out from Jess."

"You know I don't like you sleeping with her - but she's been useful. Find out where he'll be."

"Okay, if you want me to. But why?"

"I know how we're going to get rid of Bobby."

CHAPTER 40

Mags was in the hallway when Gabe arrived at the ICU. "Tip's airway swelled." She looked haggard. "They're putting a tube in his throat because he can't breathe. Oh, Gabe, to lose him ...." Tears welled in her eyes. "We've had so many good years. It may be selfish but I want more."

Gabe masked his fear and put his arm around her shoulder. He spoke with a confidence he didn't feel. "They know what they're doing here, Mags."

The curtain opened and two young women in scrubs emerged. The second one held out her hand. "I'm Dr. Baxter, the Intensivist for the unit. "You're Dr. Tipton's family?"

"I'm Margaret, his wife, and this is our friend, Gabe Wakeman."

"We had to intubate him to protect his airway from the swelling. The ventilator is breathing for him. We sedated him but he may be awake enough to know you're here."

"Will he be alright?" Mags asked.

"His reaction to the antivenom is rare but the treatment for this is well established. We're giving him medicine to quiet his immune system. He's older and he could develop an inflammation in other organ systems. The next thirty-six hours are critical. I'll be here all day and we will call you if anything changes. You can ask the nurses to page me if you have any questions."

Mags nodded in response but there was a lost child underneath her calm composure. Gabe wondered what it would be like to have the support of a woman as loving as Mags in his life.

Tip's face was parchment pale and he had dark circles under his eyes. He couldn't speak with the tube in his throat.

Gabe took his hand and tears streamed down his face. A thousand words couldn't hold the love he felt.

Gabe ordered breakfast and called Vince from his regular table at the TLT to tell him he'd brought Bobby home and fill him in on the adoption.

"I can't believe it," Vince protested. "George and I were partners for years and he never told me. Does Dana know?"

"Yes, it was a family secret. Mildred adamantly denies that Bobby is adopted or had a twin, but I've spoken with his birth mother, Louise Ruston. She lives in Laguna Beach and she's come down to find him. They're talking."

"This is a shock," Vince said. "I can't get over George not telling me about the adoption."

"Are you and Shelly ready for Chad's intervention? I'm planning to be at your house at one tomorrow."

"We'll be ready. I called the place that treated him last time and they're expecting him. Chad's truck was gone when I got up this morning, but Shelly says his girlfriend was here last night. He'd damn well better come home today." Vince ended the call.

Clare brought Gabe's Schrodinger Scramble and sat down to talk. "Is Dr. Tipton improving?"

"We thought so, but he developed an immune reaction to the antivenom." Gabe described his condition.

"You sound very clinical, Gabe. The truth is you love Tip and you're terrified of losing him."

"He's fathered me in a way my father couldn't. He's been my rock." They both fell silent.

"Did you and Louise find Bobby Wyring?" Clare asked.

"Yes. They drove back from the Ritual together. He feels like he's finally found where he belongs and she needs another son."

"Do you think Bobby is still in danger?

"We don't know who killed Neil but Louise says Jessica Wyring is sleeping with another man."

"She and her lover want Bobby out of the way?"

"Marco is suspicious."

"Family secrets are dangerous, Gabe. Be careful."

CHAPTER 41

Harrar left Dana sleeping soundly. She murmured, "Jack?" in
sleepy protest when he pulled his arm out from under her, and
rolled over.

"I'm going to my place for clean clothes," he told her.
"Get some sleep. I'll be back and we'll go over our plan."

He couldn't let Dana find out about Hayley. She was
vicious. He didn't kid himself. She'd dump him if he became a
liability and he had too much invested to risk that happening.
Hayley was a screwup he had to take care of without Dana
finding out. Hayley had witnessed him dumping Chad's body in
the back of his truck. If she went to the cops … but she hadn't
called them last night. She'd hot-footed it to Chad's apartment
instead. Then to a house in La Caya. He'd slept badly, thinking
about her reasons. When he figured her out, he almost grinned.
The bitch thought like he did: Chad had a going business. He
undoubtedly kept drugs and money in his apartment. She'd
gone to get his stash. Did she plan to take over his clients?

Harrar approached his apartment complex cautiously, but
there was no sign of police activity. He changed and bagged his

stained clothing. Better to stay at Dana's for now. He bought coffee at a drive-thru and tossed the damning clothes in a trash can on his way to the freeway. He took the 56 exit off the 805 through busy morning traffic to the inevitable jam-up going into downtown La Caya. It hadn't taken much to work out that the address Hayley had Ubered to last night was her parents' house. They lived on a leafy street uphill from La Caya Boulevard in the Gull Rock area. He parked under an overgrown Jacaranda, where he could tip his mirror to see the house, sipped his coffee, and waited.

Hayley's parents lived in a two-story California Revival with ornate ironwork on the windows. The neighborhood was dead and there was no activity inside or out. At nine-thirty a figure passed in front of a downstairs window, but no Hayley. He was about to give up and find a restroom when one of the garage doors opened and a lime-green Scion backed out with Hayley at the wheel.

He'd had an eternity to think over his options. None of them were good. The Scion turned downhill and rolled past his parked truck. Hayley was oblivious, using the rear view mirror to put on eyeliner. She went south on the Boulevard to the Gull Rock commercial strip and parked at a Starbucks. She got out of the Scion, lugging a big straw purse and a laptop, and went inside.

Harrar debated. He needed a pit stop. She'd made him wait so long he was ready to pee in his shoes. It had been dark when he was chasing her at Chad's. Would she recognize him if he went in?

His bladder made the decision. He parked close beside the boxy Scion and followed Hayley inside. Business was light. There were a handful of customers, several with laptops. Hayley had hers open on a round table and was intent on the screen. Harrar gave his order to one of the fresh-faced baristas behind the counter and went to the restroom. When he came out Hayley was returning to her stool with a cup in her hand. The barista called *John* the name Harrar had given and waved. Harrar tensed, but Hayley's gaze slid across him, disinterested.

Harrar carried his cup outside to his truck. The space between the passenger door of his truck and the driver's side of her Scion was narrow and the high bed of his truck effectively blocked the view to the coffee shop window. He started his truck so that he could lower his window and cracked his door open. He was sweating. He could smell the tension pouring off his body. Attacking Chad's bitch here was a crazy risk, but he had to shut her up. He undid the baggie with the rest of Chad's crystal, shook some into the fold of his index finger and thumb and snorted hard. He felt the rush explode in his brain.

When she came, he was gloved and ready. Clattering across the concrete parking lot in flimsy platform sandals, her arms weighted with the oversized purse and a tote containing the laptop. She activated the lock from a distance and set the tote on the concrete to open the Scion door. Harrar let her slide inside, drop her purse on the passenger seat, and reach outside to pick up the tote, before he moved. He opened his door and was standing in the narrow space between their vehicles before she could close the Scion door. He wrapped a hand over her mouth, pinning her back against her seat before she understood what was happening. She let out a stifled cry that was lost in the normal bustle of street sounds. Her protest died into the thick fabric of Harrar's work glove as the blade of his knife angled upward under her ribcage and punctured her heart.

Hayley flopped limply toward the passenger seat. Harrar hauled her upright so that she was resting on the steering wheel. He kept his head low, grabbed Hayley's straw purse and the tote with the laptop and closed the Scion door. He backed into his truck, levered himself across the console into the driver's seat and put his truck in gear.

A customer emerged from the Starbucks and paused in the August glare staring in his direction. Harrar released his hold on the gearshift, swearing inaudibly while seconds ticked by. He was so close …. The customer put on his sunglasses and crossed to a car three spaces from the Scion and Harrar dared to breathe again.

CHAPTER 42

Gabe took his anxiety about Tipton to the Tiger Lotus Dojo in Las Palmas to meet Marco for MMA practice. They sparred together on Sunday afternoons when Gabe was in town and Marco's work schedule allowed it. Working up a sweat burned off some of Gabe's edginess. Bobby Wyring was being cooperative, but he hadn't provided Marco with any new leads on Neil's death.

Marco left to take Maureen and the kids shopping. Gabe came home and showered. He was at loose ends and too worried about Tipton to concentrate. He quashed an urge to call Sam, he didn't know her well enough to interrupt her Sunday afternoon, and she'd said she wanted to take it slow.

He carried a pile of books and a bottle of water out to the patio, hoping that reading would settle his mind. A few pages in, the irrigation came on and a geyser of water arced head over his head from a broken sprinkler. Gabe rescued his book and got out his tool box and a shovel to repair it. At six, he changed out of his muddy clothes, showered again and walked back down to the TLT for dinner.

Mac had ramped the ceiling fans up to full power to clear away the aura of the hungry crowd that had packed the TLT all weekend. He and Sylvie had a game of Stratego open on the bar. Sonny was clearing tables and Chuy could be heard belting a Roberto Carlos ballad at full volume while he scrubbed a towering collection of pans. Mac interrupted his quest to outmaneuver Sylvie long enough to duck into the kitchen and bring Gabe a platter of Chuy's Sea Bass Hoja Santa.

Gabe was inhaling the mixed aroma of lemon and mint with anticipation when Bobby Wyring came in the door with Louise Ruston. Gabe raised a hand in greeting as Mac led them past his table.

"Thanks again for all your help, Gabe." Bobby shook his hand. "My mother and I have a lot of catching up to do."

"Years of it," Louise agreed with a wide smile, "I can't thank you enough, Mr. Wakeman." They followed Mac to an empty booth.

Gabe noted that they were meeting on neutral ground. What was the atmosphere at the Wyring's house today? Had Bobby found out about Jessica's lover or had she learned about Erin?

Mac delivered water and menus to Bobby and Louise. He touched Gabe on the shoulder as he passed. "Those two friends of yours got trouble ahead. Y'know, things that look good can make problems, and vice versa. That boy doesn't know the half of it yet." He went back to his game, leaving Gabe staring after him.

"I suggested meeting here because Jess and I aren't getting along." Bobby told Louise. "We were up arguing until 3 A.M. She's pissed off because I was stressed out and stayed at the casino instead of coming home. I haven't told her about you yet. We're keeping our differences from the kids – Susan's seven now and Jake is five. You're going to love them, Louise. They're smart as whips. Hard to believe they have cousins they don't know about … I don't even know their names. There's so much to take in."

"I can't wait to meet your family," Louise said. "You look so much like Neil. Your left eyebrow goes up the same way when you talk."

Bobby aligned the menus with the edge of the table with meticulous attention and averted his gaze. "Why did you give me up and not him?" His voice quivered.

"You keep coming back to that. You have to understand how it was." Louise's tone was conciliatory. She didn't want to lose Bobby now that Neil was gone. "I wish I'd had the courage to keep you both but I was working as a waitress and just barely making ends meet. I couldn't manage two babies and the Wyrings were wealthy. Adoption was a way to give you a better life."

"You picked him instead of me." Bobby clung to his grievance.

Louise ignored him. Thirty years of shedding her shame and becoming a woman had toughened her. "Mr. Wakeman was convinced that you and Neil were connected. When he was killed, I came to Santa Linda and Gabe helped me find you, Bobby. Maybe with time I can show you I love you."

Harrar was parked in one of the diagonal slots at the side of the TLT. He slumped low in his truck seat with the AC on and the driver's side window open, blowing a thin stream of cigarette smoke into the hot air while he waited for Bobby to

155

come out. Jessica's text had put Bobby meeting Louise at the TLT from five to seven. Bobby appeared at the door and Harrar flicked the butt of his Marlboro into the street.

Bobby and Louise got up from the booth and hugged each other awkwardly. "I'll talk to Jessica and maybe we can meet together at my house tomorrow," Bobby said.

"I hope you work it out soon. I'll be at the Oceana waiting for your call. You go ahead, I want to use the restroom before I leave."

Louise faced herself in the restroom mirror. Threatened tears had smudged her eyeliner. She redrew it like Joan of Arc adjusting her armor for battle. Bobby's insistent questioning was wearing her down. He had torn the stitches open on buried wounds Louise would have been happy to leave alone. Bobby had never been real to her. His birth mother had sold him to the Wyring's as an infant before she'd come to Louise with baby Neil in her arms. As Slammer, Louise had no urge to be a parent. But the bloody hormones she was taking for her gender change flooded her with an unexpected rush of maternal feelings. She'd adopted Neil as his mother and he'd become her entire life for thirty-five years. He was dead and Bobby was her only chance to be a mother again.

She bade a polite goodnight to Mac and stepped outside the TLT in time to see Harrar backing Bobby into the driver's seat of his Sequoia at gunpoint.

CHAPTER 43

Louise ran back inside the TLT in disbelief and went immediately to Gabe. "A man with a gun just forced Bobby into his truck! We have to stop them!"

Gabe was on his feet in the time it took her to speak. "Did you see who it was?"

"Big, buffed guy. My car's at the curb." Louise bolted toward the door with Gabe on her heels.

"Don't let them out of your sight!" Mac shouted, "and for god's sake be careful." Louise hit the lock and Gabe jumped in the passenger seat. She accelerated up the street. "That's them turning uphill." Gabe pointed. "They're taking Sheffield to the freeway. Stay behind them. Not too close. That guy has a gun and we don't know what he'll do to Bobby if he's threatened. I'll call my sheriff friend, Marco Brandt."

Gabe pushed speed dial and counted the agonizing rings before Marco's voicemail kicked in. "Marco. It's Gabe. A guy carjacked Bobby Wyring at gunpoint outside the TLT. Louise Ruston and I are in a white Camry. We're following Bobby's silver Toyota Sequoia with California licence plate WYCO2.

They're headed north on the 5. We just passed the 78 offramp. I'll text you with updates."

"Where are we going?" Louise asked.

"No idea. They're moving into the right lane. They're taking the 76. There's a lot of wild country east of the 15. Brush and Indian reservations."

"A good place to dump a body," Louise trod on the gas and the car jumped ahead.

"Easy!" Gabe said. "Our only advantage is that they don't know we're behind them. Keep some cars between us and them and hope Marco picks up my message."

"The man with the gun could be the one I saw in bed with Jessica."

"The same man who stabbed Neil and chased him into the train, thinking he was Bobby? It doesn't make sense. Divorce is easier."

"All I know is, he killed my son," Louise kept the Sequoia in sight.

"They're crossing the 15 and continuing east. Just stay back." The landscape transitioned from housing developments into avocado groves.

Gabe's phone chirped, "Amigo? I got your call. I was coaching Ricky's soccer game at the Polo Grounds. Where are you now?"

"We just crossed the 15 on 76 East. They haven't seen us. I think the carjacker is the Wyring's carpenter. The man Jessica is having an affair with."

"Jack Harrar? You're sure he has a gun?"

"Louise saw him force Bobby into his truck. She got a good look."

"I radioed the CHP and sheriff's office and explained the situation. They'll report the vehicle if they see it. I'll run

Harrar's name against California records for priors and be there as soon as I can."

Curve after curve of repetitious blacktop threaded between rock outcroppings and hillsides covered with desiccated summer brush unwound in front of the car. Gabe answered his phone before the first ring ended.

"Jack Harrar is on probation for a rape he committed while he was managing an apartment complex in Playa del Rey," Marco reported. "Possession of a firearm is reason to land him back in jail. Before his jail time he had a charge of GBH. Not a nice guy to cross. Keep following, but don't approach him."

"Bobby's signaling for a left turn. He's getting off the highway on a dirt trail marked Ashley Road. I think there used to be a big quarry up here that was slated for a landfill. We're going to stay back and let them get ahead of us. We can track them by their dust cloud."

"I'll ask the sheriff's department to send units. Don't get shot, Wakeman. Backup is on the way."

CHAPTER 44

Dana was sitting on a flat rock under a desiccated eucalyptus when Harrar and Bobby rolled slowly to the quarry's edge. The plume of dust trailing the truck settled and Harrar ordered Bobby to turn off the engine and lower his window.

Dana loved the expression of dazed astonishment on Bobby's face when he saw her. Dumb wit. He'd never been as quick as she was. Let's see how long it took him to realize he couldn't charm his way out of this one. Golden Boy. Always perfect in their parent's eyes and sneaking around to get more. Now Mildred was going to give him all the money. Not while she could help it. A lifetime of resentment blistered in Dana. She could taste bile in her throat as she approached the driver's side window of Bobby's truck. "Put your arm out," she demanded.

"Dana! What are you doing here? What's going on! Jack sticks a gun in my side and tells me to drive or else. This is like a bad TV program. Have you two lost your minds?"

"Shut up!" Harrar jammed the barrel of the gun under his jaw. "Put your arm out the window like she says and keep your other hand on the fucking wheel!"

Bobby stretched his neck away from Harrar and complied." You can't do this!"

"I can do anything I want to." Dana had to stand on tiptoe to reach Bobby's arm. She jabbed the hypodermic she was holding into the back of his arm and pushed down the plunger. Bobby yipped and jerked, but the gun barrel stopped him.

"You bitch! What was in that needle?"

"Mother's insulin."

"That could kill me! Why are you doing this!"

"Why do you think? You suck money from Mother that's mine. Every week you wheedle more of my inheritance out of her, and now she's cutting me out of the will."

"It's your own fault. If you were nicer to her, she wouldn't do it. this is crazy, Dana."

"She's never loved me. All she can see is you."

"You can't get away with this. Just let me go and I'll split everything with you. I promise.

"That's a fat one! I wouldn't trust you, ever."

Bobby started to tremble. The insulin was taking effect. His face went blank, his neck stiffened, and his eyes rolled upward. He slumped toward Harrar. A line of drool trailed from the corner of his mouth.

Harrar pushed him upright and Dana laughed. "Jesus Dana, you must really hate him."

"He ruined my life."

"Take this. I've got to get rid of our prints." Harrar handed Dana the gun and began wiping down the truck's interior.

Bobby arched forward and vomited on his shirt. Harrar avoided the mess and started the truck. He put it in neutral and got out. "I've got to wipe the outside doors."

"I want to see him go into the quarry."

"You're sure the water is deep enough to cover the truck?"

"We came out here to party when I was in high school. We used to dive in it. There's a spring; it never goes dry."

Bobby moaned.

"Hurry up, Jack!"

Louise and Gabe drove down the dirt road too slowly to raise dust. "Stop in that bunch of trees," Gabe told Louise. "They're parking at the edge of the quarry. What's Harrar up to?"

There's a woman out there!" Louise pointed. They watched the small figure rise from the rock and walk up to the Sequoia.

"Wait in the car. I'll go ahead on foot and see if I can get close. Call Marco." He handed Louise his phone and got out.

"Give me a hand. This thing is heavy." Harrar told Dana.

The Sequoia began to move. Dana walked around the rear and spotted Gabe dropping behind a creosote bush. "Jack! There's someone here!" She yelled and fired at Gabe. The shot went wild and she fired again. The truck rolled toward the quarry.

"Stop shooting and give me the fucking gun!" Harrar grabbed at her arm.

"Marco? This is Louise Ruston."

"Where's Gabe?"

162

"Bobby's truck is parked at the edge of a quarry at the end of Ashley Road. There's a woman with Harrar and it looks like they intend to drive it over the edge. Bobby's inside and Gabe's gone out there to try to stop them."

"He's crazy to go out there if Harrar's got a gun!"

"Where are you? We need help!"

"Stay where you are! I'm sending units to your location."

"Hurry up!" Louise watched Gabe zigzag behind bushes and rocks, closing in on the truck. Bobby's kidnappers were pushing the truck toward the quarry. Gunshots shattered the simmering August afternoon. A pair of ravens exploded from a ghostly eucalyptus on the quarry's edge. The truck was rolling inexorably toward the lip of the quarry with Bobby in it.

Louise started her car and floored it across the field toward the Sequoia. The Camry wasn't made for off-road driving. It bottomed out on holes and rocks. The car launched into the air and came down with a jolt. Louise's head hit the roof. She kept the gas pedal on the floor and tore on. She'd lost Neil; she'd die to save her other son.

Another gunshot. The windshield spider-webbed into glittering fragments in front of Louise's eyes. She slammed into the wheel well of the rolling Sequoia in high gear. The front of the Camry crumpled. The air bags smacked her against the seat and the world went black.

CHAPTER 45

The crash gave Gabe time to dive behind a rock. Short, black hair, not
Jessica. Dana Wyring. Bobby's sister.

Three shots that sounded like a .38. If it was a revolver Dana had two rounds left. Gabe chanced a look. The truck had stopped moving. Steam billowed from the hood of the Camry. He couldn't see Louise. Dana was standing clear of Bobby's truck, pointing the gun toward the rock Gabe was hiding behind.

Harrar had been knocked to the ground by the impact. He picked himself up. "Give me the gun!" He advanced on Dana, dragging his left leg. "You can't hit shit and we've got to finish him."

Dana faced Harrar. The barrel of the gun didn't waver. "Fuck you, Jack." She fired. "You're no use to me now."

Sirens screamed faintly in the distance. Harrar grunted and toppled over. Blood bloomed on his shirt. Gabe couldn't tell how badly he'd been hit.

Dana walked toward the rock that sheltered Gabe. Four shots. Gabe gripped a baseball-sized rock in his hand. He stood up and hurled it at Dana. It hit her mid-chest. She cried out and hunched over in pain. The gun hung loosely from her hand for an agonizing moment.

She brought it up again and fired, but pain from the blow had ruined her aim. The bullet whanged past his head. She pulled the trigger again. The gun clicked on an empty chamber.

Gabe rushed her before she could react. He wrenched the gun out of her hand, tossed it hard away, caught her arms, and flipped her in the dirt face down. He was sweating and he could feel his heart thudding in his chest. He kept her immobilized with a knee in her back.

The sirens were on top of them. Screaming in his ears. Coyotes answered in kind. Two sheriff's cars skidded to a halt in a cloud of dust.

CHAPTER 46

"You look worse than I do, Gabe." Tip said. He was sitting up, off the ventilator. There was a breakfast tray pushed to one side and he'd regained some of his normal contrariness. "I want to get out of here and get some real food. "Did you find Bobby?"

"You were right about the casino. I found him there but he escaped. I also found his birth mother. It's a bizarre story." Gabe explained what had happened while Tip was out of it. "Louise is okay and they're keeping Bobby for observation. Dana and Jack Harrar are in custody. They're probably ratting on one another while we're talking."

"Did being shot at set off your PTSD?"

"Hard to say. I had a few hours of decent sleep last night. I've been so activated with all of this I haven't had time to unpack it." Being shot at hadn't rattled Gabe the way seeing Neil's body cartwheeling in front of the train had. The psychic scars of helplessness are specific. His impotence to prevent Neil's death was a replay of his helplessness at not being able to save his co-pilot in Columbia. Tipton had helped Gabe see his pattern but it was up to him to change it. He had to accept that the only person he could save was himself.

"Let's meet tonight and I'll help you reestablish your calm center. You know the drill."

"No so fast." Mags jumped in. "For once you are going to listen to your doctors and rest, Joseph. Just last night we weren't sure if you were going to pull through."

"She's right, Tip. I'll be okay. Maybe for a little while you can let me take care of you."

CHAPTER 47

Gabe's phone rang as he was leaving the hospital. *Marco.* "Where are you?"

"Visiting Tip. He's off the ventilator and clamoring to go home. Mags has been scared as hell and won't let him leave til his doctors say he's safe. What's up?"

"I have bad news, amigo. Chad Conklin is dead. Dana and Harrar are blaming each other. It's not clear who's responsible yet, but he's dead. His parents are clients of yours, right? I need someone to deliver the news to his family. I can send a unit over there but I think it will be better if they hear it from you.

"Shit." Gabe pulled over to let the news sink in. "I helped them do an intervention on Chad last year. He's been running off the rails again, using and dealing. We were planning to get him back into rehab." He drew a heavy breath. "You're sure there's no mistake?"

"I wish there was, but we found his body. A kid like that had everything and a good life in front of him. Fucking drugs."

Gabe knew Marco was thinking of his own brother who'd died dealing drugs in the streets of Miami. "I'll go to the Conklins now. They should hear this from me."

Gabe found himself in the slow lane on 5 North. He was in no hurry to see Vince and Shelly. He'd left them worried and angry about Chad's disappearance. Those feelings would be buried in their grief.

Gabe drove up the long hill to the Conklin's, recalling Bobby's tail lights speeding into the darkness. That was nine days ago; it felt like years.

Shelly greeted him at the door. Her hair looked slept in and she wasn't wearing makeup. "Thanks for coming, Gabe. We still haven't heard from Chad. Vince is in the kitchen. Coffee?"

Gabe plastered a neutral expression on his face. "That'll be good." He followed her down the hallway into the sunny kitchen. Shelly had decorated it with bright colors and cheerful knickknacks to assure herself that life was always sunny. Vince was hunched over the local paper, a forgotten coffee cup at his elbow. Gabe sat down across from him.

"There'll be no intervention," Vince growled at Gabe. "The little asshole hasn't shown.

"No, that's what I've come about. Why don't you take a chair," he told Shelly, who was hovering uncertainly with cups in her hand. "I have bad news."

Shelly sat down and started to cry.

There wasn't any easy way to tell them.

"Marco asked me to come. I'm afraid Chad is dead. "

Shelly let out a long scream and was silent.

Vince stared at Gabe, the expression on his face shifted from anger to despair. "You're sure about this?"

"The police found his body this morning. Dana Wyring and Jack Harrar have been arrested. They think they're responsible for Chad's death." He told them what had happened.

Shelly moved closer to Vince and he put his arm around her. Both were crying.

Gabe took Shelly's hand and opened his heart to their sorrow.

CHAPTER 48

Bobby sat down on a metal bench in the shade of the hospital portico to wait for his ride. His head hurt and his legs were shaky. He was too exhausted to deal with Jessica. She'd go apeshit when she heard that his sister had enlisted their carpenter to kill him. She hated Dana and she'd never shut up about it.

His Uber arrived with the stereo blasting Arabic rock. The car smelled vaguely of sandalwood and there were crocheted doilies pinned to the headrests.
The driver's head was bobbing in time with the music. "You are Mister Bobby? You are going to Seaside?" he shouted.

"That's me." Bobby climbed in the back seat. "Would you turn that down please? I have to make a call." He needed to tell Mother that Dana had been arrested before she heard it on the news.

"Wyring residence."

"Janie, it's me. I need to talk to Mother."

"She's napping now. Can you call her later?"

"Damnit, Janie! Dana tried to kill me and the police have arrested her! She injected me with Mother's insulin and shot the guy who was helping her. They're both in jail."

"Dana tried to kill you?" Janie repeated the words as if he was speaking a foreign language. "Bobby, are you okay?"

"I've had a hell of a time. Dana and a guy who works construction for us kidnapped me and took me out to the old quarry where we used to party in high school. They shot me full of insulin and were going to roll my truck into the quarry with me in it. My birth mother, Louise, rammed her car into the truck and saved me. My friend, Gabe Wakeman, tackled Dana and got the gun. They took me to the ER at Lowell Memorial but I'm fine."

"Your birth mother?" Janie echoed.

"Yes!" Bobby was impatient. "Louise Ruston, my birth mother. Get with it, Janie! Do you hear anything I'm saying? Give Mother the message."

"Where are you?"

"I'm on my way to the Lonesome Threesome Bar and Grill in Seaside. I'm picking up Louise and we're going to meet the sheriff's detective there."

CHAPTER 49

The noon rush was past and the TLT was quiet. Gabe was at his usual table and Marco was seated across from him. They each had an iced tea. Sonny was tending to lingering diners while Mac and Sylvie solved the daily crossword on the bar top and pretended not to eavesdrop. Marlowe was seated on a stool next to them staring at the paper. Gabe imagined a pen in his paw.

"What's a thirteen-letter word for Masquerade," Mac asked the room.

"Concealment?" Gabe offered.

"Not enough letters," Mac said.

"Impersonation," Sylvie was confident and the cat yawned.

Gabe smiled. Life was normal at the TLT. He tore open two packets of sugar and stirred them into his glass in an effort to kick start his brain.

"You look like hell," Marco said. "How did it go with the Conklins?"

"You know how that goes." Gabe felt the weight of exhaustion behind his eyes. "It's never easy."

"I swear you've got nine lives, Gabe. You gotta stop using 'em up."

"If Dana hadn't run out of bullets, I'd be dead."

"I'm glad you're still here. I'd miss our workouts."

"How are Bobby and Louise doing?"

"Louise was released, but they kept Bobby in the ER for observation. We questioned Louise this morning but I need to take Bobby to the station to get a formal statement. I suggested he meet me here."

Louise and Bobby arrived together. Bobby looked haggard and Louise had a black eye and swollen cheek. She'd tried to cover the bruising and failed. Bobby slid out a chair for her and they said their good mornings. Sonny asked if they wanted coffee. They both looked like they needed it.

"Is Dana talking?" Gabe asked Marco.

"She called her attorney and he stopped her talking." Marco said. "She blames everything on Jack Harrar. She says she was afraid of him and he forced her to inject Bobby with insulin."

"That's complete bullshit," Bobby was incensed. "Dana hates me."

"It was all about money," Marco said. "She claims she deliberately missed Gabe and Louise and shot Harrar in self-defense. Dana thought your mother was going to change her will and leave everything to you so she wanted you dead. Dana used Harrar to do her dirty work. She sent him to the Surf Fair to kill you, but they didn't know you had a twin and he stabbed Neil by mistake."

"She deserves to be locked up forever."

"She's a nasty piece of work, but she cries convincingly. A jury is going to love her."

"Gabe and Louise saved my life," Bobby said.

"You're a very brave woman," Gabe told Louise.

Marco nodded in agreement. "You're the queen of the demolition derby. If that truck had gone over the edge Bobby wouldn't be here. That quarry is a hundred feet deep."

"I wasn't going to lose another son," Louise said. "Dana was shooting at Gabe and I stepped on the accelerator without thinking. All I knew was that I had to save him."

"It's lucky that you and Gabe were there." Marco said. "I need to get a statement from you," he told Bobby. "It'll take about an hour."

"I'll take you to meet Jessica when I get back," Bobby said to Louise. "The kids will be home from school this afternoon."

The two men left and Sonny appeared with menus. "Lunch?"

"I'm starving," Louise said. "What do you recommend?"

"I'll have the special. What is it today?" Gabe asked.

"Relational Risotto. I added extra thyme."

"Make it two of them," Louise agreed.

"Are you going to tell Bobby that Jessica was having an affair with Harrar?"

"I don't want to spoil our relationship before it starts. Some things are
better left unsaid."

The front door of the TLT opened with a sigh. The woman in the doorway hesitated, panting heavily, as if she'd reached the end of a gangplank and could go no farther. Gabe recognized her by her blue cotton nurse's uniform, but he had no idea what she was doing here.

"You made it. Come on in," Mac abandoned his crossword and waved her inside. "Can I help you?"

"Is Bobby Wyring here? He said he was meeting a sheriff." She ran out of words and stopped with her mouth open.

Louise simply stared.

Gabe registered a shift as if the temperature in the room had changed. He crossed the floor and offered his hand. "Hi, I'm Gabe Wakeman, a friend of Bobby's. I saw you at Mildred Wyring's. He was just here and we expect him back soon. Won't you join us?"

She clutched his hand like a lifeline and plunked into a chair. "I'm Janie Syzmakowski. I work for the Wyring's." Words tumbled out of her mouth. "Bobby told me a woman named Louise Ruston is going around claiming to be his mother." Janie's voice was shaking. "She turned to Louise. Are you her?"

"Yes."

"Well you can't be Bobby's mother, because I am."

Louise cleared her throat. "You don't recognize me, Janie. I used to be Slammer, Ronald Ruston. Now I'm Louise."

Gabe watched the news hit Janie broadside. Realization worked its way across her face. "Slammer? You're a woman. You can't … But you're …"

"Bobby's father. Yes. "I was starting the change when you brought Neil to me. Neil is gone and Bobby's all I've got left. He thinks I'm his mother and I want to be part of his life."

"I've been waiting thirty-five years to tell him that *I'm* his mother. Dana's in jail where she belongs and Bobby is going to inherit Mildred's money."

"Are you counting on him to take care of you?"

"I don't need his money. George Wyring made sure that I'm okay. I just want Bobby to love me."

"That's all I want, too."

"I'm his mother." Janie's jaw set.

"And I'm his father."

The two women were deadlocked over Bobby, the golden boy, who'd never been required to put anyone else's needs before his own. Each woman had a confession to make. Gabe began to speak and stopped. He could hear Tip's voice. *This is not your problem.*

He hadn't noticed Sylvie slide down from her stool and depart as silently as her cat. Clare came in carrying a single plate. "Bobby will be back soon," she announced with authority. She set the plate in front of Gabe. "Louise's hotel is just down the street, Janie. You two need to go over there and decide what you're going to tell Bobby. Now, come on." Louise rose without objection and Janie followed her meekly.

Clare saw them to the door and came back and took the empty chair across from Gabe. "I think you've had enough of other people's problems. What have I missed?"

Gabe told her the story of Bobby's rescue at the quarry.

"Is getting shot at part of your job description?"

Bobby is my client and I feel responsible. I couldn't let them roll him off into the quarry in his truck. Besides, my psychological struggle is resolved. I finally got to save somebody."

"What you've always wanted," Clare laughed. "Saving someone lets you feel better, Gabe, but it's a false solution. Until you sort out your compulsion to act as a savior, you'll keep attracting people who need to be rescued."

"Amen to that," Mac called from the bar.

"Did you ever figure out the meaning of your counting vision?" Clare asked.

"Three. Four. Five. Those were the last bullets Dana had in her gun. The vine saved my life. My vision told me I needed to count the shots to know when she was out of bullets and I could tackle her."

"You're learning, Gabe. It's time to take care of yourself," Clare's voice was warm. "Enjoy your lunch before it gets cold."

"Yeah," Mac agreed. "Why do ya think you came in here in the first place?"